Even Villains Fall In Love

LIANA BROOKS

OTHER WORKS

HEROES AND VILLAINS

Even Villains Fall In Love
Even Villains Go To The Movies
Even Villains Have Interns
Even Villains Play The Hero (books 1 – 3 omnibus)
The Polar Terror

TIME AND SHADOWS MYSTERIES

The Day Before
Convergence Point
Decoherence

FLEET OF MALIK

Bodies In Motion
Change of Momentum
For Every Action (forthcoming)

SHORTER WORKS

All I Want For Christmas Is A Werewolf
Darkness and Good
Fey Lights
Prime Sensations

Find other works by the author at www.lianabrooks.com.

EVEN VILLAINS FALL IN LOVE

LIANA BROOKS

AUSTRALIA

Print ISBN: 978-1-925825-93-0
eBook ISBN: 9781513000671

www.inkprintpress.com

National Library of Australia Cataloguing-in-Publication Data
Brooks, Liana 1982—
Even Villains Fall In Love
128 p.
ISBN: 978-1-925825-93-0
Inkprint Press, Canberra, Australia
1. Fiction—Superheroes 2. Fiction—Romance—Science Fiction

Summary: Theoretically-retired supervillain Evan Smith must decide which he wants more: the world, or the woman he loves.

Second Edition: May 2015
Cover Artist: LFD Designs
Editor: Deadra Krieger

A SPECIAL THANKS TO:

The Slackers, Dreamers, and Tweeps who helped me get this far my four ice cream minions whose antics inspire me daily my husband for always being my hero

CHAPTER ONE

I knew from the first time I saw my wife that I wanted her naked. Of course, seven minutes later I wanted revenge. It wasn't that she had handed me my first defeat or ruined my chances for world domination that year, it was the way she kissed me goodbye. She sent my head spinning, then walked away as if I were the least important person in the world.

Once my arm healed, I stole some new equipment, cloned some new minions, and I felt a little different.

I wanted revenge, with a side order of naked.

ACROSS THE DINNER table, Tabitha devoured him with dark, ocean-blue eyes. She put a bite of lettuce in her mouth, full lips pursing around it. Eating salad never looked so good. Her tongue darted out to lick away a stray drop of dressing. She winked at him, promising with every move to do the same to him. "It's almost bedtime," she said, her voice husky and luscious.

"I don't wanna go to bed!" one of the quads screamed.

"What about cake? Don't we get birthday cake?" another asked.

Evan winked back at his wife from the far side of the table, separated by a few feet and four precocious just-turned-five-year-olds, all as stunning as their mother with big, round eyes and hair that fell in loose curls meant to trap hairbrushes and sticky substances. He had to peek at the eyes to see who was talking. Maria had green eyes, Angela's eyes were blue like Tabitha's, Delilah's eyes were brown like his, and Blessing—their stillborn who miraculously survived—had purple eyes. The waif in question had blue eyes.

"Angela," Evan said, "after dinner it's pajama time, and then story time."

"Mommy doesn't have a bedtime!" Angela wailed, shoulders drooping.

Tabitha winked at him again. "Tell you what, tonight Mommy will go to bed the same time you do. Right after we eat cake." She leaned over to give Angela a hug.

All Evan could see was the deep V plunge of her tight blue shirt.

Oh, yeah. Crime didn't always pay, but altering someone's moral compass sure put the O's back in the bedroom.

The cake was split into fourths, equal parts purple, white, green, and blue so each girl could have her favorite color in the cake. Baking four cakes was unreasonable; there weren't any grandparents left to celebrate with, and neighbors had an annoying habit of asking uncomfortable questions. Saying little things like, "You look just like Doctor Charm! Do you remember him? Whatever happened to that guy? Do you know how hard it is to put together a good Villains vs. Heroes fantasy league without him?" made for awkward evenings.

So they had a quiet family party. Cake, then presents, after which he hurried the girls off to bed so he could read Dilly Duck's ABCs in record time before rushing to the bedroom, hoping to catch Tabitha still in the shower.

She was already out and wearing a blue satin robe that caressed her skin in exactly the way he wanted to. Rose-scented candles cast sensuous shadows on the walls.

Tabitha turned, lips curved in an inviting smile. Long fingers twined with the sash of her robe. She tossed her honey-blonde hair in the way she always did when she was about to argue, posing with feet apart and one hand casually resting on her waist. "Sweetie, we need to talk."

Evan wiped grease-stained hands on his jeans as he forced a smile. "Sure, babes, anything you want."

"Really?" She slunk forward, all sinewy limbs and doe eyes. "Promise?" Tabitha nuzzled his nose.

One hand flirted up the back of his neck to play with his hair. The other traveled downward, right to his zipper.

Oh, yes, the little Morality Machine in the basement was working just fine. Another thirty, maybe forty years of this and he'd consider retiring. Or turning the machine down so his wife wasn't quite a sex kitten every day of the week. Maybe only days with Y in them.

"Sweetie?" She nibbled his ear. "I want to go back to work."

"What?" Evan actually pushed himself away from her, something he wasn't sure was possible in any other circumstance.

Tabitha tucked her chin and pouted.

"Tabby-cat, I love you, but work? I've got my... stuff... in the lab. I'm busy. And we can't afford daycare for the girls. We're barely making ends meet as it is. Do you really want to go back to being Zephyr Girl? Crime fighting is a game for the young, baby. You're not nineteen anymore."

"I'm twenty-nine. A very"—her hips pressed against his tight jeans just so—"very healthy twenty-nine."

He shivered at her touch. "You're cheating."
"I want to do this, Evan." She ground against the thick denim.

"You can do me all you want, baby."

She stepped back, frowning. "I'm serious."

"So am I." Evan sighed, reaching for his wife. "Sweetie, I love you, but what's the point in being a superhero? The government stipend barely covers the dry-cleaning bill. If it's money you want, write another tell-all superhero book. The Spanish Mask sold his third last month."

Tabitha crossed her arms. "I don't want to write another book just for royalties while you're between jobs."

He waved a finger at her. "I'm not between jobs. I work freelance in the computer business. I'm self-employed. That's not the same as being between jobs."

"Between paychecks then."

"We will have a solid income. This project I'm working on, Tabby-cat, it's going to set us up for life. We're never going to worry about money again. I promise. Give me a couple of weeks and everything is going to be perfect." He caught her hand and pulled her into his arms. The faint scent of her spicy perfume left him dizzy with need.

She rested her head on his chest. "I want to save the world. Have you seen the news, Evan? An entire town in Kansas held hostage for a week by a bomb scare before a superhero was able to get in to defuse the situation. A week! I could have that done between grocery shopping and paying the bills. Ten minutes, no pulling punches."

"I know, baby. No one is better at this stuff than you. But I need you at home, Tabby. Having you out there scares me. I'm terrified I'd lose you. Why don't you wait until I finish this project? I'll be done by the time the election rolls around. Two more weeks. Once I get paid we'll look at this again. I have that armor design for you, I just need some time to put it together."

Tabitha sighed. "You've been saying that since we got married."

"Well, my nights are busy." He nibbled her ear as he tugged her sash loose. "Are you complaining?"

Tabitha stretched against him, sending a delightful frisson of lust up his spine. "I thought you gave up the super villain schemes."

He twitched. "I did, baby. Of course I did."

"But you're keeping me here. Isn't that a little selfish? Just a teeny-tiny bit super villain-ish?" She slipped her hand between his pants and his skin.

"Ah!" He caught her hand so he could think clearly. "Not selfish. Necessary. Like oxygen or sex."

"Don't you mean water?"

"No, definitely sex." Evan slid her robe off and tossed it into a corner. "Come here, Tabby-cat, I'll make you purr."

She tugged at his shirt, pulling it up.

The shirt joined the robe on the other side of the room.

"What are you doing down in that lab?" she asked as her hands drew lazy circles on his back.

Ten seconds, that's all he'd need to get her panties off. Three more to drop his pants. "What was the question?"

"What are you doing in the lab? What's this project?"

"Oh, computer stuff. I told you. To help tally everything on election night. I'm trying to make the process run smoother so we don't have to worry about recounts."

"Hmmm." She gave him a dubious frown.

Tabitha was built like a supermodel and had a superhero name straight from Campy Comics, but her brain was Mensa all the way. "And this computer program has nothing to do with world domination, or get-rich-quick schemes?"

Evan contrived to look wounded. "Tabby-cat, how can you ask that?"

"Because you spent ten years as a villainous criminal mastermind?"

"I wasn't a mastermind, I was a super villain, there's a difference. Masterminds are just thugs with money. My crimes had artistic flare. I was practically Robin Hood! Robbing from the rich and scandalous, and giving to me."

"Robin Hood gave to the poor," Tabitha said with a laugh. "You were never poor."

He caught her hand, pulling her close. "Poor is relative. Besides, I'm reformed now. You showed me the error of my wicked ways. Although"—he leaned in for a kiss—"if you'd like to remind me why I gave up a lucrative life of crime, I have the evening free."

CHAPTER TWO

Someday, I know the kids are going to ask for the story of How I Met Their Mother. Every kid asks; it's a rite of passage like losing a tooth or learning to ride a bike. I just don't know how to tell them without losing their respect.

The truth is, Tabitha broke into my lab and kicked me and my minions clear into the next time zone. She can move at sonic speeds even when she's not flying. She blew past my machines like they weren't even there. Embarrassing, of course, but that wasn't the worst part. No, the part that will make my daughters lose all respect for me is how, while their mother was kicking my rear, I couldn't take my eyes off hers. Not when she wore a skin-tight white bodysuit and bustier on the verge of a wardrobe malfunction. Any man who can think straight when confronted by that must have a wonderful boyfriend at home, because I've seen drag queens hand in their Prada kitten heels for a shot at Tabitha.

EVAN WOKE UP relaxed and ready for another dose of marital bliss. Let the bachelors have their one-night stands, lost to the alcoholic haze of the weekend. Married life meant getting lucky three or four times a day, when dentist appointments and world domination didn't demand his full attention. He rolled over and reached for Tabitha.

She wasn't there. "Tabby? Babes?"

"In here!" she called from the closet. He relaxed back into the Tabitha-scented sheets. "What do you think?" she asked, stepping out of the closet in her white Zephyr Girl bodysuit: reinforced leather leggings, gloves, and bustier. Knee-high, steel-capped boots and a sky blue cape completed the outfit. Tabitha hovered, the air around her seething with the aurora borealis that always accompanied her use of super powers.

"You look amazing." She'd looked like that first time he'd seen her. "Come here."

She flew to him, settling over the bed before dropping the last centimeter. "It still fits."

"I know." He caught her lips, tasting her.

"Do you know where my trench coat is?"

"In the hall closet." He reached for her hair, but she was already gone.

A breeze slammed the bedroom door open and shut. Tabitha cinched the belt to her white trench coat around her tiny waist with a smile. She sauntered away with her hips swaying to pull her purse out of the closet, along with a pink scarf.

He shook his head as she slipped past him to the door. "Wait! Tabitha, where are you going?"

She froze in the act of putting on sunglasses. "Work, remember? We talked about this. I'm going to work; you're going to take care of the kids. Right? Good. I'll try to be home by seven. Make sure dinner is ready."

The front door slammed shut on Evan's bewildered expression.

Tabitha swung the door back open. "Sweetie? Get the lawn service out here, the yard looks like a jungle, and hide the crayons. The girls found where I was keeping them yesterday. I don't want them coloring on the walls again."

Shut. Open. "Love ya!"

"Um..." Evan ran to the front lawn and watched his wife leap into the sky, flying away to save the day like any good superhero with a deadline. This was not a good thing.

Back inside, Evan scrambled to find jeans in the mountain of unfolded laundry.

"Daddy?" Delilah said through a yawn.

"Yes?"

"I want breakfast."

"Breakfast?" He stared at his daughter. "Um, let's see what Mommy left."

The other three girls were waiting quietly in the kitchen.

"I want Mommy!" Delilah said.

Blessing sat at the table with an expectant expression. "Pancakes?"

He peeked into the cupboard. There were boxes of things neatly stacked with matching lids. That probably meant something profound in the secret language of women, but he wasn't even getting a mixed signal.

"Daddy?" Four judgmental scowls looked up at him. "Can you cook?"

"For a given definition of cook." He closed the cupboard door. "Give Daddy a minute." Evan ran through the garage to the door to his basement lab. "Hert!"

His warty toad of a minion climbed up the stairs, six-knuckled fingers dragging on the floor. "You bellowed, Master?"

"Do you cook, Hert?"

"I wasn't programmed to, Master."

He'd forgotten that. Hert was his original minion, a summer project cooked up from the DNA of animals he'd been able to find in his backyard when he was fifteen and had nothing better to do with his life. Back then, Mom had cooked.

In college he'd had the meal plan. Tabitha did the cooking once they got married. Back in the bachelor years between college and marriage...

"Girls! Get dressed. Daddy's going to take you to McDonalds!"

Angela put her hands on her hips, posing just like Tabitha. "Fast food is very unhealthy for you. Mommy said so."

Evan looked at his warty minion for help.

"Never hurt me," Hert said, shrugging.

The girls wrinkled their noses in unison, a move worthy of the synchronized snob team at the country club he didn't belong to.

"I don't want to look like him," Maria said.

"Daddy survived on fast food before he met Mommy." Evan dropped his head. He was arguing in third person with five-year-olds, a sure sign of senility. "This is not part of the plan," he muttered to Hert.

Tonight, the Morality Machine was getting a tweak. It might mean some extra late nights in the lab after Tabitha fell into a satisfied slumber, but sex would keep her home. Although spending eight hours a day making love wouldn't actually get the kids fed. "Everybody to the car."

The girls watched him with intent glares.

"There will be toys."

CHAPTER THREE

Superheroes were new to our world when I met Tabitha. No amount of theorizing, wild supposition, or unethical research revealed to science where their powers came from. Even I couldn't figure out what twist of genetics or fate controlled those powers, and believe me, I tried.

My interest in Tabitha may have started out as one hundred percent lust. I couldn't forget her kiss, the taste of her on my lips. Eventually, the lust dissipated a little and three percent of my fascination was with her power. I didn't care about the rest of the superheroes. I just wanted to know how Tabitha worked.

She can fly. She moves faster than any human should be able to. And she makes the world glow. Maybe I'm biased on that last one. When she's with me, everything seems brighter.

"WE CAN'T DO this, Hert," Evan told the minion as he tried to pull the lab door closed. Maria pushed her foot between them as she tried to peek down the stairs.

"I don't see what else we could do, Master," his minion answered. Two warty arms stretched across the opening to keep the girls at bay. They were a little taller than his favorite minion, and didn't seem too worried about the closet monster who'd eaten breakfast with them.

"I'm not programmed for nurturing or caregiving, sir," Hert reminded him. "It's not in my DNA. If you give me a week, I could work out the sequence to clone a nanny."

"We don't have a week. Not a week's notice to clone a minion, and not a week I can sacrifice in work time. It's almost November."

"We could slow time," Hert suggested. His foot bounced up to keep Delilah from crawling under his arm.

Blessing tugged on Evan's pant leg. "Daddy, can I go downstairs?"

"Now, sweetie, what does Mommy say about going to the lab?"

Folding her arms, she pouted. "Not unless Daddy's with you."

"Right. Is Daddy in the lab, sweetheart?"

Blessing tilted her head to the side in an exact imitation of her mother. He needed to win the election. If nothing else, he needed the Secret Service guarding his girls before they went to school.

"Daddy?" Blessing asked. "Will you go to your lab? Please?"

Evan groaned in dismay. "That's cheating!"

"We could put them to work, Master."

"There are child labor laws," Evan said. "Even if I ignored the laws, what could they do?"

"Sort widgets," Hert said promptly. His daughters danced around him.

"Fine. Girls? We are going to Daddy's lab. Only touch something if Daddy says it's okay. Understand?"

"Yes, Daddy!" they chorused before rushing Hert like the offensive line at the Pro-Bowl and charging down the stairs.

"Hert?"

"Sir?"

"Keep them away from the machines."

"Yes, sir."

"And the knives," Evan said as he hurried down.

"Yes, sir."

"And the blow torches."

"Yes, sir."

"And the screw drivers."

"Yes, sir."

"And the electrical outlets."

"Yes, sir."

"And the drafting pencils."

"Yes, sir."

"And the lasers."

"The lasers are out for Minion Field Day, sir."

"Hert?" Evan said as the girls ran into his lab and stopped next to the Agree-With-Me Ray with appreciative 'oo's' and 'ah's.'

"Sir?"

He looked at a lifetime of notations on a collection of whiteboards, lines of meticulously maintained tools for his engineering projects, and glowing vats waiting for his next minion. "Keep the girls away from everything."

"Yes, sir."

Evan took a deep breath of the cold laboratory air and all his neurons began firing. Here, surrounded by diagrams and machines, he wasn't the geek caught flat-footed who didn't know the answer or how to make pancakes. In the lab, he reigned supreme, ready to mete out swift judgment and tackle everything.

On the far side of the room, nearest to the subterranean exit, sat his new machine: the Election Ray. The Agree-With-Me Ray's older, better-looking brother, the Election Ray didn't need close proximity to work, it just need waves of some form. Airwaves, electric waves, radio waves, and cell phone waves all worked to project a single message throbbing into the unsuspecting minds of humanity.

Early results were promising. For the first test, he'd sent a message encouraging everyone to buy purple Banala Babes Dolls. Stores had sold out, but only of red and blue. People had bought the dolls in pairs and hadn't touched the purple. Fine-tuning was in progress.

The rebuilt Agree-With-Me Ray sat in another corner under bulletproof glass. He had fond memories of that machine, but the original was too bulky for use as anything but a museum piece. A smaller version shaped like an obsidian statue of the Greek goddess Nike sat beside the first, also under glass. Three industrious minions were working on the latest version as per the specs he'd drawn up the day before—all the power of the original Agree-With-Me Ray streamlined to fit into a stylish wristwatch.

"Daddy?" Delilah ran to him. "What's a widget and when can I sort one?"

"Hert!"

"Master?"

"Give them something to sort."

"Yes, Master." Hert obediently found a jar of mixed screws and nuts, dumped it on the concrete floor, and sat with the girls to help them sort the contents.

Evan watched for a moment before heading to his favorite invention: the Morality Machine with its ability to adjust one fine-tuned aspect of the personality. After all, he didn't want Tabitha as a slobbering monster with no morals. As a villain, she'd be downright scary.

Love was a complicated thing, a complex process in a constant state of flux. Most people didn't understand how to perfect the three-part harmony of lust, attachment, and commitment that produced true love. He was ahead of the game there, lust had fueled Tabitha's first kiss. Even now, the memory was enough to make him harden with need. Any villain of moderate intelligence could whip up a basic love potion to produce lust—a combination of adrenaline, dopamine, norepinephrine, and serotonin. But, like any bad cocktail of drugs, there was a time limit on chemical mixes. The body eventually adjusted and then love faded.

Third-stage love involved free will and commitment. He couldn't take away Tabitha's free will without risking her mind entirely. Driving down the street, she might need to swerve suddenly to avoid a deer or oncoming car. Without free will, she wouldn't be able to protect herself.

So he'd focused the machine on the second stage of love: attachment. Mad lust kept the bedroom games fun, but attachment made sure she only wanted to play with him. His machine focused magnetic waves on the glands that controlled production of vasopressin and oxytocin. A second magnet sent a pulse wave that triggered memories of their time together. It was as good as staring into her eyes for hours at a time. Tabitha lived in the soft glow of fond affection, always thinking of him.

If it weren't for the Morality Machine, their first kiss would have been their last. Tabitha would have found some other man, someone she didn't instantly write off as beneath her. She would have found love the old-fashioned way, and he would have died of a broken heart.

The core of the Morality Machine winked at him under the spotlight. Such an elegant machine. The black matrix around the crystal looked like a spider web lain out by MC Escher. The crystal heart shone translucent blue and showed the perfect moment: Tabitha kissing him.

The image wasn't part of the machine, more a screen for what the machine did. Tweaking it would be hard. With the proper fix, he could boost her sex drive, tinkering with the first stages of lust. If he did that the crystal image would probably change to one of their more erotic forays into emotional expression, and that would leave Tabitha panting with need every hour of the day.

Who was he kidding? He wouldn't let her out of the bedroom like that! Super powers be hanged, he'd find a pair of cuffs and... Evan took a deep breath. Later.

Election Ray first. Sex later. If he turned it up right now she'd come home, and he needed to get some work done.

"Daddy?"

Evan jumped out of Angela's way. "Yes? Why aren't you sorting widgets?"

"Is that Mommy?" She pointed at the crystal.

"Yes, it is. Isn't she pretty?"

"Why do you have a picture of Mommy in the crazy spider web?"

"Because I love Mommy, and I want to think about her while I work," Evan said as he steered his precocious child back to the pile of unsorted screws.

"Where's my picture?"

"What?"

"Mommy has a picture. Where's my picture? Don't you love me?"

The other three girls gasped.

"You don't love us, Daddy?" Blessing asked.

"Of course I love you!" Evan knelt down as his brain raced to dig himself out of this hole. They were too much like their mother. Far too perceptive for his peace of mind. "I didn't have the pictures I want of you," he said slowly, constructing the lie as he went. "Why don't you girls color Daddy some pictures and we can hang them up for me to see every day?"

Maria clapped. "Can we decorate?"

"Sure, why not? Hert, do we have a decorating minion?"

"We have several programmed for color awareness and spatial reasoning, Master. Those are useful tools for programming."

"Great, bring one of them over." Evan plopped Delilah in his lap while the girls showed him the funny shaped things from the jar—mostly scrap metal—until Hert shuffled back over with a black and purple polka dotted minion. Like Tabitha's canisters upstairs, the color codes had made sense at one time, but now he couldn't remember why he'd programmed the genes for polka dots. Maybe he'd been drunk at the time.

"Master, this is Fishy Thing."

"Fishy Thing? That sounds like one of my high school projects."

"Yes, Master. You programmed Fishy Thing during your senior year."

Purple and black. That's right, he'd meant it to look like the homecoming game with everyone in school colors. "Great. Fishy Thing, my girls want to decorate. Help them out and keep them away from the machines and anything else dangerous. Understood?"

"Yes, Master," Fishy Thing answered.

He checked on Agree-With-Me the Third, then went to work fine-tuning the Election Ray. The plan was the epitome of simplicity. Everyone knew the president of the United States was the most powerful person in the world. Power, influence, acclaim, wealth, attention... everything Evan had ever wanted rolled into one. But becoming president meant close public scrutiny, lying on a daily basis, and a year of hard work as he tried to build support for his lies. Unless, of course, everyone happened to want to write his name in the box for president on Election Day.

Evan would win by a landslide. One hundred percent of the vote without rigging the system.

There couldn't be an argument because everyone would want him to win. The Election Ray ensured they would justify why they voted for him. He merely needed to fine-tune it a little bit, and keep Tabitha from finding out.

Bad timing on her part. Did she really need to go back to superheroing now? Not that she would leave him, the Morality Machine kept that from happening, but she'd be upset. And then he'd feel guilty.

But really, he thought as he started dismantling the wave device to adjust the controls inside, this would put her out of a job. Everyone would agree with him. Everyone would obey the laws. Everything would be just the way he wanted.

CHAPTER FOUR

There are days I miss being Doctor Charm. I loved the attention and the challenge of being a super villain. Any thug with a fist can rob a little old lady in an alley. That doesn't take talent or brains.

But I was never a thug, or a don, or a mastermind. Small-time wasn't my style. I didn't want to be another fish in the pond, even if I was a big fish. I wanted to be the apex predator of the hemisphere. And I was.

EVAN PATTED HIS Election Ray. "We'll test this first thing tomorrow." If the calculations were right, he was one speech away from the Oval Office. Stretching, he turned to see the rest of his lab covered in pink and purple streamers. Crayon-scribbled graph paper covered most of the wall. Good thing no superhero was likely to stop by for a midnight battle of good versus evil, or they'd have died laughing. He lifted a multicolored paper chain off his computer. "Girls, Daddy's fortress of evil looks different."

"We decorated!" Angela said happily. "Now you have pictures of us so you can love us." She shoved a piece of paper at his knee.

Like a good father, he inspected the balloon-headed, noodle-limbed figures and pronounced it a masterpiece. Tacking the picture over a diagram of a magnetic shield he'd been meaning to build, he smiled at the girls. "Let's get some dinner going."

"What are you making?" Maria asked.

"Reservations," Evan said.

"Pizza!" Delilah squealed. Her sisters wasted no time picking up the refrain.

"In that case, I'll make a phone call." Evan shooed them upstairs, then headed into the kitchen to scrub the machine grease off his hands as he told them to turn on the TV.

"Daddy! It's Mommy!"

He turned to see Zephyr Girl smiling for the camera. She hovered inches off the ground, her hair in a ponytail, auroras ribboning around just like they had this morning.

Evan licked his lips. Tabitha had worn her hair like that last week while they worked in the garden. Her shirt had clung to her glistening skin. He'd tangled his fingers in her hair so he could run his tongue along her neck. He remembered how she shivered, her sweet coo of anticipation, the oak's rough bark scraping against his back when he pulled her close...

"Why did you come back?" a reporter asked as she shoved a microphone in Zephyr Girl's face.

"I thought it was time. There was no real reason behind this, simply a desire to do good."

The reporter pulled the microphone back. "And with your return, do you expect to see the return of your arch nemesis Doctor Charm?"

Zephyr Girl laughed. "I don't think anyone needs to worry about Doctor Charm. I handled him the last time we were together."

Only Evan knew to look for the slight tweak in her smile that meant Tabitha was talking to him.

She'd handled him all right. She handled, he'd gone down, they'd both hit their peaks. Maybe tonight she'd be interested in the fondle variation, or a replay of the events in slow motion.

"And what can we expect to see from the new and improved Zephyr Girl?" the reporter asked.

"Me at my best, saving the world!" She tossed her hair, mugging for the camera and fueling a thousand adolescent dreams. With a wink, she shot off in a cloud of sparks.

"Why does Mommy get to fly?" Blessing asked.

"Because Mommy is special," Tabitha answered from the front door. A breeze fluttered her white cape.

Evan smiled. "Hello, beautiful."

In a blink, she was in his arms, warm and safe. She stood on tiptoe, kissing him as she had the first time. "I missed you," she said. He caught her hand, keeping her from turning away as the girls tugged at her cape and peppered her with questions.

"I'll go make dinner," he whispered in her ear as he watched a bead of sweat pearl on her neck and slip down her cleavage.

He wanted to run his tongue down her neck after it and then head lower. His jeans tightened.

Tabitha stretched. "I'm out of shape. I forgot how much work it takes to fight."

"Sore?"

"Everywhere!"

"I'll give you a rub down tonight."

Blue eyes went wide with desire. "Promise?" she nearly purred.

"Promise. I'll rub everything."

By the time Evan returned from tucking in the girls, amber and amethyst candles lit the bedroom. He locked the door and watched candlelight dance across his wife's bare skin as she lay on the black satin sheets, like an offering to some ancient god. Golden hair flowed like a molten river over her pale skin. Evan slipped onto the bed and kissed a thin white scar on her upper arm. Flying glass in the lab had cut her the first time they'd fought. He'd realized then that he could never win against her. Every bruise on her body tore him apart.

Running his fingers down her back, he savored her scent and her quiver of anticipation. Evan smiled and leaned down to whisper in Tabitha's ear, "Do you really want a back rub?"

"To start."

Taking a bottle of lavender oil from the nightstand Evan warmed it in his hands, and massaged the knots from her back. She hissed in pain and he lightened his touch. "What did you do today?"

"Git Kraken was terrorizing Key West with his latest genetic constructs."

Evan chuckled. "Really?"

"Truth is stranger than fiction. Apparently he was offended that he wasn't invited to host a drag queen beauty pageant."

He caressed her, basking in her presence like ancient man worshipping the first goddess. "This is the man with tentacles, isn't it?"

"That's the one. He has tentacles and ego, but not much else." Tabitha rolled to the side and stretched a long leg onto his lap. "My hip is sore."

He obediently focused on her hip, watching her body melt in pleasure.

With a languid sigh, Tabitha rolled to her back. "Mmm. Evan, I was thinking of something this morning."

"So was I," he said, his voice low and smoky.

"Really?" She pushed up on one arm. "Have you thought about where to go?"

"I was going to start here." He moved one hand inward of her hip. "Then work my way down—"

She swatted his hand away. "I meant a job, Evan."

He frowned. "You went to work today, sweetie, what else is there?"

"I want you to get a job!"

"I have a job."

Tabitha rolled her eyes. "You lock yourself in the basement and fiddle with a computer."

"It's a job."

"I want you to get out of the house. You need friends."

"I have friends."

"Minions don't count."

"If I can watch movies with them, they count."

Tabitha propped herself on her elbows. "Look at me." Her nipples peaked in the cold air, begging for his attention.

"I am."

"You're wasted in the computer field. Why don't you go work at the university? You'd make an amazing teacher."

He lifted his eyes to her face. "Would you stay home with the girls if I went to work?"

"Is that the only way I can get you out of the basement?"

"Yes."

"Why don't you want me at work?" Tabitha frowned. She sat up and crossed her arms.

"I don't want you hurt." He traced the scar on her arm. "Do you remember this?"

"It was a scratch."

"You don't heal fast, Tabby-cat, and I can't risk losing you. You have too much of me. Without you I would fall apart."

"No you wouldn't. You're a handsome man, you'd find someone else." She flopped back in the bed with a sigh. "All you have to do is smile and women trip over themselves to have you. Last time I let you go grocery shopping someone wrote her phone number on the minivan with shoe polish."

He chuckled. "There's only you, love. Always and forever, only you." He leaned down and kissed her. "As I recall, it took more than a smile to catch your attention." He nudged her over so he could finish her backrub—and think. "Would you really give up Zephyr Girl again?"

"Until the girls start school. If you taught morning classes, you could be back by the time school was out."

He fingers found a subtle dent in her skin where stretch marks had left their tracks during pregnancy. She'd hated the eighty pounds she gained carrying quads, but he'd loved her full form, almost missed it some days.

That was an idea. "What if we want another baby?"

Tabitha laughed. "No."

"A little boy?"

"Couldn't we adopt?"

"We could, but I'd miss the libido boost from the second trimester."

"Tell you what," Tabby said, flipping over. "Take your clothes off and I'll fake it."

With a grin, he unbuttoned his shirt. "You have to fake it with me?"

"Every day," she said, putting a dramatic hand to her forehead as she laughed. "It's an absolute *chore* trying to fake all those orgasms."

"I hate to make you work. I'll let you off to-night." He dropped his shirt and reached for his pajamas on the nightstand, still folded from the day he'd bought them. Eventually, he'd actually wear them.

Tabitha caught his hand, pulling him down to the bed. "Kiss me."

CHAPTER FIVE

At fifteen, power was my first love. It promised me the world—if I could only break the shackles of a wholesome middle-class up-bringing where ambition came second only to defying the home owner's association in terms of evil.

Ambition was my fatal flaw. Sometimes good ideas got ahead of me. A plan would come together and I would be in the middle of everything before I stopped to ask if this was right or wrong or even possible.

I tinkered with the Agree-With-Me Ray for years. It was a toy, really. Something I pulled out when I needed things to go my way. That changed when I saw the report about the millions of dollars in stolen, embezzled, and otherwise illegally obtained cash floating around, and realized, "It should be mine."

I turned the Agree-With-Me Ray on high and started making phone calls. A quick, amiable conversation and the thief bundled the stolen money in an envelope, sent it to my house, and forgot any of the above had happened. A perfect plan—until I cold-called a superhero.

For some reason, I never learned to regret that mistake.

MANICURED FINGERNAILS DRAGGED up Evan's spine. He arched, rubbing against satin sheets, and rolled over to capture his wife. "I thought you were going to work."

"Nothing is going to happen before eleven," she promised. A wicked smile curved her lips. "At least, nothing bad." She darted forward, teasing him with her tongue before retreating. Pale morning light played across her skin, throwing luscious curves into shadow and highlighting her golden tresses.

"Tease." He pulled her close so he could feel the heat of her body on his. "How do you know nothing will happen?"

"How do you know a piece of coding will work?"

He traced the curves of her body, committing every soft, sensuous turn to memory. "I just do."

"That's how I know." Tabitha's naked body rubbed him in all the right ways as she arched into his touch. "That's also how I know what I want right now."

He nipped her ear. "Right now?"

"Two or three times."

"Only three?"

"Maybe a few more in the shower if the girls don't wake up."

"And one for the road?" he asked hopefully.

"Maybe. If you're up for a marathon."

He chuckled and rolled onto his back, pulling her on top of him. "Staying up for you will never be a problem."

Tabitha flew away at a quarter after ten, leaving Evan feeling limp and hungry for more. Science liked to prove that the average man possessed only limited abilities. That was probably true, but Tabitha had a voracious sexual appetite, and he'd learned to keep up with her.

He lay on the bed, watching the ceiling fan turn slowly, thinking about his long to-do list. For some reason, images of Tabitha stretched out under him kept invading.

He wanted her against a wall tonight while she was wearing that pair of high heels he'd bought her last month. And then they could take a bubble bath. Mmmm, slipping his hand across her body in the water was always fun. A touch of his finger and she'd be begging for more. He could tease her until she was incoherent with need. And then—

"Daddy!" Blessing screamed from the living room.

Evan rolled off the bed and pulled his clothes on. His jeans were easier to put on without Tabitha around. Not to mention the lust killing effect small children had on him. "What is it?" he asked as he tripped over a fluffy unicorn.

"Daddy, I'm bored," his youngest announced in funereal tones from the middle of a sea of stuffed animals and building blocks. "Delilah locked me out of the toy place."

"The toy place?" He kicked a path through the disaster and sat on the old blue couch, confused.

"Your toy place."

Evan looked across the living room to the garage door. "You mean my lab?"

"Yes!"

"The door was locked." The door was always locked. It kept minions from running across Tabitha's path. If too many showed up Tabitha might start wondering why he needed all those minions.

"Not for Delilah," Blessing said.

That was not a good thing. He rushed the stairs and found that the door was unlocked. "Delilah? Sweetie?"

"Daddy!" She bounced at the bottom of the stairs, squeezing a furry, red minion like a stress ball. "Can we decorate more?"

"Sweetheart, how did you get the door open?"

She shrugged. "It wanted it to open. I went click"—she snapped her fingers—"and it opened."

"Click?"

"Uh huh. Watch!" She sauntered over to his locked cabinet of power tools. "Click!"

The door swung open.

"Oh, boy." Evan stared at the door for a moment, letting all the implications sink in. His eye twitched.

"Let's not tell Mommy about that little trick. Okay? Just in case we need a back-up plan for college funding." Evan grabbed her hand. "Look at me, sweetie. Do not click locks unless Daddy says so. Do you understand?"

"Okay."

Evan ran his hand through his hair. "Well, on the bright side, you have a future as a locksmith, or a super villain. I'm not sure Mommy is going to like that."

"I'm going to be a superhero," Delilah said. "Just like Mommy, 'cept my suit's gonna be purple."

He frowned. Keeping the villain aspect of his life secret from his family made sense, but there were moments he felt he ought to spend a little more time corrupting the children. Doctor Charm, father of four superheroes? He'd be the laughingstock of the super villain underground.

"Daddy?" Delilah patted his arm. "Can we have pancakes?"

"Sure." Even super villains could make pancakes. If a former mafia don could get his own cooking show, Evan could make pancakes. They came from a mix. Just add water—like sea monkeys. Although the last batch of sea monkeys he'd made hadn't turned out well. Pancakes were easier, he assumed. Less prone to eating red sports cars, for one thing.

He chased the girls upstairs and shouted over his shoulder for the minions to start putting combination locks on everything.

Two hours later, he had everything under control to the point where he could go back to the lab.

"Master?" Hert said, a clipboard clutched in his claws.

"Yes? If this is another request for a Caribbean cruise, the answer is still no. If you get one, Tabby will want one. If Tabby goes, I need to, and then the girls will want to come. I'll never hear the end of it."

"The neighbors took their dog on a cruise," Hert pointed out, a touch offended. "But that wasn't why I needed you. I have the latest popularity polls, Master."

"Excellent! Is everyone still failing?" he asked eagerly. "Anyone with over 50 percent of the vote might give me problems. I need my win to look plausible to our international neighbors; a popular candidate would ruin that illusion."

"A failing you've mentioned several times, Master," Hert said as the lab door squeaked open.

"Yes." Evan perused the Gallup Polls. "Good. This is good. I think we're still on track."

He glanced up as Delilah and Blessing approached the Morality Machine. "Girls! Stay away from that! Hert, go look after the sprouts, please. I need to get the machine calibrated. Are we getting any results from this morning's test run?"

"Nothing positive, Master," he said as a second minion ran up with the purchasing results. They were less than promising. Ideally the Election Ray would focus the victim's thought on one particular object. His tests had sent them after dolls, or shoes, or newspapers. On Election Day, he would persuade the voters to focus on his name so they would write it on the ballot, because no matter what people said, crime never paid as well as politics.

"Master?" The blue minion who'd brought the results quavered at his feet. "I have some correlating data that you may find intriguing."

Evan gestured for it to continue. "By all means, intrigue me."

"The results of the ray are more pronounced when they side with an observable trend."

"So it's working better when people are already thinking positive thoughts about the subject?"

"Yes, Master."

"Good to know, but not helpful."

"You could make a large donation to a charity on TV the night before election," the minion suggested. "Or perhaps save a bus full of children."

"I don't make public appearances. Too many people want me for questioning. And buses never are in danger when you need them to be."

"We could arrange for the danger, Master. Such a small matter..."

Evan glared at it. "None of that! I'm charming. I persuade people to give me what I want. I insinuate myself into their lives. I don't threaten them. Threatening is for thugs."

"Yes, Master." Slumping, it slouched away.

"We'll find another way," Evan said. "All I need is for them to have one thought: Evan Smith for president. Once we can transmit that message, the rest is taken care of."

Hert pursed his pale lips. "We could change the output from persuasion to pure suggestion. It wouldn't be as subtle, but we could loop the message."

"Distance hypnosis?" Evan drummed his fingers on the worktable. "I'd need to switch the tertiary capacitor to handle the energy load, but it could be done." He nodded. "Let's break down the machine and see if the magnet can handle the phase change."

CHAPTER SIX

Tabitha bewitched me. I dreamt of her, pursued her in a way I'd never chased after a woman before. Usually, women came to me. Even villains have standards, and no one can boast about forcing a woman. Brute strength doesn't have the delicious flavor of well-performed seduction.

The Morality Machine didn't compel, it just lowered her inhibitions. A superhero in bed with the villain? I can think of few things more taboo. Under the influence of the Morality Machine, Tabitha was perfectly herself—utterly confident, always in control—but living with the constant suggestion that she wanted me in every way possible.

EVAN BENT BACK over the Election Ray. "Hert! I need a hand over here!"

"At once, Master." Hert hurried over.

"Help me get the logistics box out. I must have something moving on the wrong frequency. It's days like this I wish we lived near a college. What I wouldn't give to have a live test subject from the correct demographic nearby."

"Do you wish me to unlock the wi-fi again, Master? I'm sure some geek will wander by to borrow it."

"Tempting—"

Glass shattered on the far side of the room. Evan moved before he'd even processed what had happened.

"Girls?" He grabbed Delilah's hand, looking for blood. "Are you okay? What did you do?"

Tears trembled in Blessing's eyes. "I wanted to see Mommy!" Blessing cried. "I smashed Mommy!" She clung to Evan's leg, sobbing at his kneecaps.

Evan pulled Delilah and Blessing close, away from the busy minions sweeping up glass, as he tried to process what happened.

The Morality Machine was broken. Pieces of the miracle that made sure Tabitha loved him were scattered at his feet. Conductive fluid, red as blood, seeped from a slashed tube.

He licked his lips. Words escaped him. Not sure what else to do, he picked the two girls up. They were real, solid, something that would ground him in the here and now.

No matter what else happened, Tabitha would never leave the girls. But still, he'd never turned off the machine. Even with the girls, he'd considered it too risky. There were too many variables for him to accurately calculate the possible results.

Theoretically, Tabitha wouldn't change much. She'd be frostier. Inhibited perhaps, inattentive, less forgiving and more likely to question what he did in the lab. Superheroes were defenders of the right; they adhered to a strict moral code. One that didn't involve villains.

She thought Evan was reformed though. That might buy him some time. As long as she didn't find out what he was doing in the lab, she might not notice he'd lied to her about his day job. Oh, sure, the sex might taper off for a few nights, but nothing too drastic. All he needed to do was fix the machine. This was a minor setback, a few hours of work. Nothing he couldn't fix.

Taking a calming breath, Evan walked in a circle around the broken Morality Machine. He couldn't even tell what had happened. For destruction this catastrophic, it didn't compute. There were safeguards, redundant features. He'd had the minions try to destroy the machine before he originally turned it on. The thing was built like a tank.

"Sweetheart, what did you do?" he finally asked. Scaring little girls was what super villains did, not the loving husbands of superheroes.

"Blessing tried to pick it up," Delilah supplied. "But it got stuck."

He looked at the little girl in his arms. She was tall for her age, but not tall enough to reach the crystal focus that floated in a magnetic field six feet off the ground. "How did you try to pick it up, sweetie?"

"I thinked about it, Daddy. Like when I want water. I think about it, and it comes to me."

"Uh huh." Evan set Blessing on the ground. "Can you think something else over here? A pencil maybe? Or a cup?"

Blessing nodded with a stoic look on her face. She scrunched her eyes shut and Hert's clipboard floated toward them, hovering to a halt inches from his nose.

"I see." He rubbed the stubble on his chin. "Telekinesis. That's going to make life fun. Later, Daddy will show you how to pick up all your toys by thinking." As soon as the election was over he was going to dedicate himself to finding out the genetic mechanism for super powers. What he wouldn't do for telekinesis!

"That's not fun!" she protested, and the clipboard clattered to the floor.

He smiled. "Cleaning never is, but it still needs to be done. Now, Delilah, how did the crystal get stuck, and what did you do?"

"I clicked it, Daddy."

"Clicked it?" Evan frowned at her. "I thought we agreed you weren't going to click anymore. Clicking is bad."

"But Blessing wanted to see Mommy!"

"Then you should have asked Daddy. I have other pictures of Mommy." He took a moment to center himself and refocus. The idea that the Morality Machine might break had never invaded even his worst nightmares.

"Daddy?" Delilah asked, tugging at his sleeve. "Are we in trouble?"

He studied his broken machine. There were probably worse things that could happen, like an asteroid the size of Mars crashing into the Pacific Ocean, but on a scale of one to ten this was a thousand. "Just a little bit."

The anguished wails of the unjustly accused began again. Delilah sobbed, clinging to his knee like a limpet. Blessing's lip trembled.

"Everyone upstairs!" Evan ordered. "Hert, salvage what you can, then send a cooking minion upstairs."

"Do you still want me to lure in a test subject, Master?"

"No, that's on hold for now."

"But, sir! Your deadline!"

"A few hours won't hurt anything," Evan said, as much to himself as Hert. He needed to fix his Morality Machine, but first he needed to figure out exactly what the girls could do. Plans boiled in the back of his mind. It was like opening the cupboard and finding a gold mine. Super powers might turn out to be the magic wand that could fix everything.

Of course, the ethics involved with using children as evil minions was sketchy at best. It probably went against child labor laws. But that was neither here nor there. All he had to do was wait for them to hit their teens and order them to not rob the bank. Kah-ching!

Upstairs, Evan lined the girls up on the couch and paced. "All right, ladies, it has come to my attention that you've been keeping secrets from Daddy. Now, as a super villain—*former* super villain—I can understand your need for secrecy. In some cases, I will applaud it. For example, I will never need to know what partially digested food looks like, so kindly don't regurgitate on me.

"However, I do need to know if you are developing any skills that might make your kindergarten teacher scream next fall. This is very important. Delilah can click things open. Blessing has telekinesis." He raised an eyebrow at the other two. "Any more surprises for Daddy?"

Maria looked at the ceiling, then the floor.

"Maria? What do you want to tell Daddy?"

"Sometimes, I make stars."

"Stars?"

She cupped her two little hands and light pooled into her palms. As she pulled her hands apart a trail of sparkling stars the size of quarters strung out in front of her.

"May I see?" He held out a hand, but waited for her to nod. Evan reached gingerly for a star. It burned hot even a hand's width away. "Do they burn things?"

"Only if I forget them, Daddy."

Oh, goody. His daughter was a firebug. "That's going to make camping trips exciting. Don't play with stars in the house. Angela?"

"Angela knows what we're thinking," Delilah offered.

"I do not!" Angela shouted. She stood up with her hands on her hips, looking exactly like Tabitha in a fighting mood. "Delilah knows everybody's secrets! Not me!"

"What do you do?" Evan asked Angela.

She shrugged a thin shoulder. "Sometimes I know when people are sad. Sometimes I make them happy."

His inner evil genius squeed like a manga fangirl at her first ComicCon. "You influence people's feelings?"

"Only a little," Angela said. "It makes my head hurt, and my tummy gets all wavy."

"Queasy you mean?"

She nodded.

"So one telekinetic, one pyrokinetic, one mind controller, and one locksmith." Evan frowned. Three high-level mutations and one limited focus telekinetic. Why didn't that sound right? "One of these things is not like the other. Delilah?"

"Daddy?" She looked up, the picture of innocence.

"Do you do anything besides click?"

"No, Daddy."

"You're sure?"

"Yes, Daddy. I don't do nothing but listen. Sometimes people tell me funny things."

"Like?"

"Like everything, Daddy. Mommy told me what she bought me for my birthday, and the man at the store told me how to get his money from the machine."

Probably a form of mind control. Uncontrolled mind control. The tiny part of his brain responsible for self-preservation and putting the brakes on really bad ideas curled into a corner, gibbering in terror.

"She does puzzles quick too," Angela offered.

"Puzzles is easy," Delilah confirmed. "They're just like locks. They want to be in order."

They weren't even in school yet! Maybe he could talk Tabitha into sending them to a private boarding school.

In the Swiss Alps.

With nuns. And absolutely no boys.

He patted Delilah's head. "This is something Mommy doesn't need to know about. She's stressed. She's had a long day at work. Let's keep all of this to ourselves until the time is right."

"When is the time right?" Maria asked.

Ten weeks after never. "When she's calm. I'll get her a trip to the spa, some flowers"—*lots of champagne*—"and tell her then. For right now..." He mimed locking his lips and throwing away the key.

The girls mimicked him.

"Good. I want you four to stay upstairs while I clean the glass up. Stay right here. Do not open the front door. Do not color on the walls. Do not move things, start fires, or hit each other. I am not explaining black eyes or ER visits to your mother tonight." Or any other night while the absence of the Morality Machine kept her stuck in the rigid black and white world that superheroes loved so much.

CHAPTER SEVEN

Superheroes make the average person jealous. The superhero mutation is the full package of charisma and power. Stunning good looks are standard, and exceptional strength and stamina are often included. Everyone wants to be special; it's ingrained in the human psyche. But there's a dirty little secret that everyone leaves out of the pep talks: for you to be special, everyone else needs to be average.

Special is just another way of saying freak.

I have no super power of my own. I don't fly. My bones break as easily as the next person's. But I do have a highly evolved brain, a certain touch of arrogance, and a naturally persuasive nature even when I'm not augmented by machines.

I've never needed anything else.

EVAN SENT HERT and two other minions upstairs to watch the girls while he worked on the broken Morality Machine. Whatever Blessing had done, she'd done it well. The crystal focus lay shattered into a few billion pieces, the tubing hung in shreds, and the magnet that did most of the work had cracked down the center. He'd spent weeks hunting down the right size magnet to trigger serotonin and vasopressin production in the female brain.

Fine-tuning the thing for Tabitha had taken the whole three-week honeymoon. Death by sex only sounded like a good idea. In practice, there was too much of a good thing. Especially if you were out of practice because the only woman in the world you were interested in was the one who walked away.

"Hert!" he bellowed.

There was a flap of webbed feet on concrete and his chief minion stood at quavering attention by his side. "Yes, Master?"

"Do we still have the plans for the original Morality Machine? I need a list of supplies."

"We can have most the supplies by the end of the week, Master. I'll need to check the specifications for a few things, and the crystal will take at least two weeks."

"We don't have two weeks, Hert. We may not have two hours." He rubbed the bridge of his nose. An almighty migraine was coming on. "Who owes us favors?"

"Sir?"

"Is there anyone we could have pick a fight with Zephyr Girl today? Challenge her to hot dog eating contest or something?"

Hert's eyes bulged in shock.

"Scratch that. Get some minions upstairs. The house needs to be spotless. Everything she's been asking for in the past month, find it and get it. New dresses in the closet, new shoes, go steal a new car if you have to."

The minion cleared his throat. "Don't you think, perhaps, that stealing might make her angrier?"

Evan sighed. "Right. Superhero morals. Wrong, right, black or white, no happy medium ever. I hate superheroes. Tabby excepted," he said before Hert could cut in. "I can do this. I can do this. Tabby doesn't know I'm still working as Doctor Charm. Maybe she won't notice." He looked at the shattered image of him holding his wife. "Let's pray she doesn't notice."

Four hours later, he was sitting in the corner of his lab, desperate for a long cool drink of something strong. He wanted Tabitha home, wanted her in his arms and kissing him, but he was terrified of what would happen when she did. He'd already packed a bag with the essentials, in case she gave him his marching orders.

"Daddy!" Blessing screamed from upstairs. "Mommy's in a fight!"

Evan whipped around. "Hert?"

"We didn't schedule anything, Master."

He took the steps three at a time. "What's going on?"

"Mommy's in a fight," Maria repeated calmly.

Picking up Maria so he could claim a spot on the couch, Evan watched as Zephyr Girl whipped around a giant lizard thing, the unholy offspring of Barney the dinosaur and Godzilla. Zephyr Girl darted in, pulling a trip wire past the reptilian legs and dodging a heavy fist. His heart skipped a beat. Right after Election Day, he was finishing the body armor he'd planned for her. It hadn't seemed necessary when she was a stay-at-home-mom, just kinky in a fun way.

A heavy green claw swiped downward, and Zephyr Girl didn't move fast enough. She bounced off a building, her neck snapping back.

"Mom!" Delilah rushed to the TV screen. Tiny fingers fanned over the live image of Zephyr Girl plummeting toward the ground. "Move back!" Angela ordered, pulling on her sister's shirt.

"Let me see Mommy." "Move, Tabby. Move, baby," Evan whispered. He hugged

Maria tighter. The TV needed to be off. Now. The girls shouldn't watch their mom die. He shouldn't watch his wife die. Anger burned through the fear. Whoever created that abomination was going to pay.

Zephyr Girl somersaulted. A burst of auroras buffered her feet from the hard cement and she shot back up. Vivid blue lights burned the sky.

"Yay!" Maria clapped as she bounced on his leg.

Zephyr Girl did a barrel roll to dodge another wide-armed punch. In a flare of light, she twisted, swung around, and punched the monster at supersonic speed. The creature staggered like an ancient redwood. Buildings shook with its fall and Evan laughed in relief. How would U.S. Geological Survey classify that kind of earthquake?

The girls clapped as Zephyr Girl waved for the cameras. "Nothing to worry about," she said with a radiant smile.

Voices overwhelmed the TV and the news crews all tried to ask questions at once.

"Mommy punched a lizard!" Delilah giggled.

"Zephyr Girl!" The Rainbow Dane ran up to the scene in a sparkling pink cape. "You're injured!" He posed dramatically.

Evan rolled his eyes. "Okay, girls. Enough TV. Let's go get dinner ready. Mommy will be home soon."

"Is Mommy hurt?" Blessing asked, trying to peek around his arm to see the TV as he moved to shut it off.

He glanced at the screen where The Rainbow Dane was wiping blood off Zephyr Girl's arm. Right next to the scar he'd left on her. That armor was getting built tonight. She'd never be hurt again.

"Mommy's fine," he promised, flicking the TV off. "The Rainbow Dane is helping her out. He'll wipe out the scratch, put a smiley face BandAid on, and send her straight home. He's a good guy, that's what he does."

"Who is The Rainbow Dane?" Delilah asked.

"Someone who is never coming to dinner," Evan muttered. He stalked off to the kitchen planning to reheat the spaghetti sauce from the freezer. On an afterthought, he went to check the BandAid supply. It was not a manly, hero-ish supply, but bravery was certainly involved. Any adult who could walk out the door with a Pinky the Silly Goose Band-Aid on them without dying of shame was braver than he.

A quick search of the depths of the bathroom cabinet gave him three plain bandages of the no-name, store-brand variety. Much better. Not that anyone would see the bandage because by to-morrow Zephyr Girl was going out to fight evil in full body armor. Possibly with flying minions be-hind her to mop up the leftovers and deal with tabloid reporters trying to get a shot of her panties.

He bit his lip. Armor. Morality Machine. Election rigging. What he really needed right now was a way to freeze time. Or a twenty-eight-hour day. Or three of him. As the spaghetti burned, he doodled out a cloning idea. Three Evans, no, better make it four. Someone needed to take care of the house. He sniffed. What was—oh.

"Girls? Does anyone want pizza?"

CHAPTER EIGHT

Crime really doesn't pay. At least, not in a regular weekly paycheck fashion. When I married Tabitha, I convinced her that I had reformed. She believed me. The Morality Machine helped matters along, but I made sure I didn't give her any reason to be suspicious. That meant finding a job. Or, since it was simpler, creating a shell company that laundered the money from my various persuasion schemes and sent me paychecks out of the accrued interest until that well ran dry.

I freelanced, scaling back my plans and running a scheme only when our funds dipped into the danger zone. Little cons that never came up on the radar.

The bank run in China? Not my fault. And I will deny to my dying day any involvement with that one bribery scandal in DC. Although it was a clever job, wasn't it?

TABITHA ARRIVED HOME as Evan dished out the

delivery pizza. He smiled anxiously, not sure what reception he would get. "Hey, Tabby, how are you?"

She ran her fingers through wind-tangled hair, jerking it nervously. "Why does everyone keep asking me that?"

"Because you took a tumble today?" He reached to help her with her cape.

Tabitha jerked away scowling. "Don't touch me. Why is everyone trying to touch me today?"

Evan stepped back with his arms raised. "Sorry. Do you want me to get you some food?"

"No. I want a shower, and some quiet, and... space. I just need some space." She stalked into the bedroom. The door locked behind her with an ominous click.

He ate dinner with the girls in silence. Tabitha stayed behind the locked door, coming out in jeans and a tight t-shirt with a college logo only after he'd sent the girls to get in pajamas. The t-shirt wasn't one he recalled seeing in her wardrobe.

"Here's your dinner." He set the plate down in front of her, leaning in for a kiss.

She turned away, still close enough for him to feel the heat off her skin, but obviously uninterested.

Evan slid into the seat beside her, resting his elbows on the table and surreptitiously checking her for bruises. "Are you wearing a different perfume?" Whatever she had on wasn't her usual blend of floral notes.

"Does it matter?" she asked grumpily. She took a bite of pizza and regarded the slice with disgust. "What is this? It tastes awful."

"It's the pizza we usually get." Evan picked up her discarded piece and nibbled. "It tastes fine to me."

"Why are we eating pizza? I can't live on junk food."

"I burnt the spaghetti," Evan said. "Pizza was easier than trying to make a new batch tonight."

She dropped her fists to her lap with a glare. "You burnt spaghetti? How? What kind of idiot burns spaghetti sauce?"

He leaned back in his chair. "Tabitha?" Name-calling was new. Even before the Morality Machine, she hadn't lashed out like that when she was angry.

The look of disgust transferred to him. "Tabitha what? What excuse are you going to make this time? I'm sure it's perfect. Choreographed and rehearsed. Everyone always has excuses, and you know what that means? More work for me. Why are you doing this to me?" She slammed her chair back, rocking the table as she stood up. "Every time I turn around there's another lie. Tell me, was any-thing you said true? Ever?"

"I love you."

Tabitha stood up, tears in her eyes. "No. You don't." She fled into the bedroom, locking the door behind her again.

Angela peeked around the corner, a stuffed cat clutched in her arms. "Daddy?"

Pulling his emotions under tight control, Evan turned to his daughter. "Hmmm?"

"Why is Mommy yelling?"

"She's just tired," Evan said with a sigh. "She'll feel better after a good night's sleep."

"Are you going to ground her for yelling? You ground me," Angela reminded him helpfully.

"Mommy's a little too big for grounding. I'm going to..." He looked around. "Do the dishes. Mop the floor. General cleaning type of things. Are you girls ready for bedtime stories?"

"Yes, Daddy."

He put the girls to bed, cleaned, and after he was sure the children were asleep, he tapped on the bedroom door. Tabitha answered it wrapped tight in her bathrobe, the bright overhead light they rarely used making the room seem cold and unwelcoming. "What do you want?"

"Can I come in? Can we talk? Please?"

She held the door open. "I don't see what we could possibly have to talk about."

Evan took a deep breath as he stepped into the bedroom. This was the tricky part. She hadn't actually accused him of anything outright, and he didn't know how much she knew. "I thought I could explain." He closed the door gently behind him.

"Explain?" Tabitha snarled. "I put my life on the line and all the thanks I get is cold pizza and burnt spaghetti? That's how you take care of me? Like I'm some stray you let in from the cold?"

"What? You like pizza. I've seen you nibble a frozen one!" Granted, she'd been seven months pregnant, and it had probably been the cravings talking, but still.

"I hate pizza," she said coldly, crossing her arms.

"Since when?"

"Since now." She swaggered up to him, arms wide. "You got a problem with that? You want to fight with me about this? Maybe tell me what I like to eat a little more? Do you read my mind or something?"

"No, I..." He fumbled for the right thing to say. Groveling looked like the only option. "I was mistaken. I apologize. Do you want me to make something else for you? A sandwich or some soup?"

"Wow," she said in a flat voice. "You really know how to show a girl a good time."

Evan fell back on the tried-and-true. He gave her a sexy smile. "I never said I was a cook, baby. But I always give you a good time when you want one."

She went rigid, shoulders back, eyes narrowed, just as he had feared she would. "Don't touch me. I don't want anyone to touch me."

"I won't," he said, holding his hands up in defeat. "Not without an invitation." He gave her a smoldering glance that worked eleven times out of ten. Nothing. "Look, Tabby-cat, I want to—"

"Don't call me that. That's not my name." She turned away, rubbing her temples.

"Tabitha, is your head hurting?" Was sudden aggression a sign of a concussion? He couldn't remember.

Her hands dropped to her side, fisting as she pivoted. "There is nothing wrong with me!"

He sucked in a deep breath, pushed his temper back down, and tried again. "I know I made a mistake."

"You bet your butt you did."

"But we have something I don't want to lose. We've had good times together. We're happy together." He smiled at her. "Think of all the good times."

The bed creaked as she sat down. "I don't remember any of that. All I remember is lies." She pulled her knees to her chest and looked at the floor, tears welling in her eyes.

Evan froze, torn between rushing to her and respecting her request not to be touched. Cowardice won out. "I'll go get my, uh, watch. I left my watch in the living room. I assume I can still sleep in the bed? The couch is a little short."

Her lips curled in a sneer. "I couldn't get paid to care what you do."

Ouch. "Be right back." He closed the door gently behind him and ran for the lab.

"Hert!" He looked around the disaster zone. Minions were carefully labeling and sorting the remnants of the Morality Machine, but his minion-and-chief was absent. "Hert?"

"Master?" Hert's bulbous head appeared from behind the bulk of the machine's base.

"Do you have everything for the Morality Machine sorted out? Can we fix it yet?"

"Not yet, Master, but the continuing tests on the election machine are going very well. I have some promising data." Hert scuttled to grab his clipboard.

Evan brushed the clipboard away. "Not right now. Is the Agree-With-Me Ray running?"

"No, Master."

"Turn it on full blast. Aim it for my room."

"Sir?" Hert frowned in puzzlement.

"It might work on Tabitha long enough for me to fix the Morality Machine. I just need to convince her to give me a second chance. She fell in love with me once, it can happen again."

Hert frowned. "It's only meant to handle simple yes or no statements, sir. I don't know if it will have the desired effect."

"I don't want desire. I want her to agree to forgive me until I get the Morality Machine fixed. Turn it on." He grabbed the watch that contained the smallest version of the ray on the way out of the lab.

The lights were already out in the bedroom and he tiptoed across the carpet. Evan could feel the faint pulse of magnetic waves. Tabitha's scent struck him in the dark—a lush promise of fantasy fulfillment. He wanted nothing more than to slip under the sheets, hear her giggle, and feel her naked body wrap around him. With a strangled groan, he dropped into bed. Tabitha moved under the covers, the sound of cotton on cotton telling him she wasn't naked at all.

He leaned over her in the darkness, put his lips to her ear, and whispered, "I love you."

She didn't answer.

CHAPTER NINE

I proposed to Tabitha the second time we met. I had spent the intervening months stalking her, searching for a weakness, and making sure she didn't already have a boyfriend. For the life of me, I could never explain why she didn't. I can only assume every other sentient being on the planet thought themselves unworthy of her attention.

They were right. Superb doesn't begin to describe my wife. She is the pinnacle of feminine creation: intelligent, generous, giving, virtuous, funny, beautiful. I dreamed of telling her about my day, conquering the world and laying it at her feet. All I wanted was her by my side, sharing every moment of my life.

TABITHA LAY BESIDE him, resplendent and peaceful in a pair of faded gray sweats. He brushed a loose hair from her face, longing to reach those last few inches and kiss her, hold her, lock her to him so the terrible fear would go away. But he couldn't, not until she gave him permission. The look of disgust she'd given him the night before had cut him too deep. Somehow, he had to erase that look.

Evan rolled away with a sigh. Nearly a day without sex. Somewhere in the murky depths of Life-Before-Tabitha he'd gone weeks without sex, months in some cases. Sometimes he'd even been too busy to smile at pretty girls, let alone get seduced by them.

Now he was hot, tight, and hungry in a purely physical way. Lying next to her without touching might kill him. Or qualify him for sainthood. Wouldn't that be awkward? Doctor Charm canonized by the Pope for not touching his wife.

With a longing look back at her, he headed for an ice-cold shower. The water managed to freeze his libido—barely. Evan stepped out with his teeth chattering and fumbled for a towel. He pulled the last clean one out from under the sink and knocked over a set of black and gold t-shirts. A too-sweet floral scent wafted up. Not Tabitha's normal perfume at all. This was the kind she would gag over when the lady at the perfume counter attacked.

He cinched the towel around his waist and held one of the t-shirts up. "Baby? Where'd you get these shirts?" He walked into the bedroom with the shirt in front of him.

Tabitha opened her blue eyes and screamed.

Evan spun around, looking for something wrong. "Tabitha? What? What's wrong, baby?"

She scrambled away from him on the bed. "Get away from me!"

He froze. "I'm away, I'm away. What's wrong? I just wanted to know where you got the t-shirts."

"Give me that!" she ordered.

He tossed it on the bed and she pulled it close like a teddy bear, breathing deeply. "Don't touch my stuff."

"Sorry. It fell out when I went to get my towel. I didn't mean... anything." How did he get into this mess? "Are you going to punish me for everything now? 'Cause if you are, may I suggest a whip and handcuffs? We've never tried that."

She swept past him with a haughty look, slamming the door in his face.

"Tabitha, my clothes are in there."

A minute later, a pair of jeans and stained white shirt hit the bed.

"Thanks." He dressed and waited for her to change.

Tabitha stepped out with her hair pulled back in a ponytail that he wanted to free her hair from, her new college t-shirt tight enough to taunt him with everything he wanted to touch, and soft, faded blue jeans he knew felt as good as they looked.

Everything about her begged for him to touch, to worship the body of his goddess. "Tabitha..." It was a prayer.

Her eyes went wide and she froze. "What are you doing here?"

"Waiting for you."

"Why?"

"I wanted to talk to you." For a given value of talk, that was true. He wanted to use his tongue on her. That was almost the same as talking.

"No, I mean what are you doing here in this room?"

"Waiting to talk to you," Evan said slowly, patiently enunciating each word.

She turned slowly, studying the room. "Why am I here?"

"Because this is your bedroom?" he guessed as his patience frayed to one last thread. "Let's sit and talk, yes?" The Agree-With-Me Ray was still pumping vibrations through the floor. It was a yes or no question. All she needed to do was not fight him.

Tabitha hesitated, then shook her head. "I'm leaving."

"Tabitha, no! Don't go. We can work this out."

She grabbed her purse and frowned at him. "I don't even know you."

Evan stared at the closed door, lost.

"Daddy?" Maria walked over and slipped her hand into his. "Why is Mommy slamming doors?"

The truth was impossible. Evan couldn't even articulate the idea. "Um, she was in a rush, sweetie. A big project." He ran a hand through his hair and choked back tears. Tabitha... He couldn't... This was a nightmare. Some horrible dream brought on by too much pizza and stress. He would wake up, roll over, and his wife would be smiling at him suggestively. If he closed his eyes, he'd be stretched next to her beneath the sheets. He'd go exploring, reconquering familiar terrain just like the first time...

"Daddy?"

He blinked. "I need to get dressed. Get your sisters up, it's playgroup day."

"What about breakfast?"

If he saw the pot of burnt spaghetti, he'd throw up. If he saw the bottle of wine from their honeymoon, he'd break it open and drown himself. "We'll buy donuts."

"Okay." Maria ran off, shouting for her sisters to get up.

He locked the door and found himself sitting on the bed hugging Tabitha's pillow. It smelled like her, a mix of floral notes and spice and something exotic that was all Tabitha. A scent he'd know anywhere. He sniffed again. And something else. Different. A sharp sweetness that turned his stomach.

He held the pillow to his face, trying to name the elusive scent. The perfume she'd worn last night. A new scent, but that was no surprise. People liked giving superheroes presents. She'd probably stopped by a college town for lunch, and someone had recognized her and given her the perfume along with a stack of t-shirts. With a sigh, he dropped the pillow.

The sound of the girls chattering in the living room told him they'd finished getting ready for the Mommy's Day Out playgroup. A hundred dollars a head and some nice ladies from the local churches would watch your kids in a moldy basement for three hours so you could keep your sanity. Evan really wanted to spend the three hours forgetting yesterday ever happened. And this morning. And maybe tomorrow.

He hit his face, trying to slap himself back to intelligence.

Tabitha was angry. Good. Fine. He knew that might happen. The Morality Machine was a calculated risk. There had always been a chance the calibration would fail, or that her basic chemistry would change. Even he couldn't build a flawless machine, although he'd never had a complaint before. Still—Evan took a deep breath—he could see why she objected. Leaving her aroused for seven years was a little unfair. He'd always meant to slowly turn the machine down and lull her into happily married life.

But that carried the risk of losing her. What if she didn't like him anymore when the machine turned off? What if he wasn't her type? Or she met someone else? Losing her was the one nightmare he couldn't face.

And now she was gone.

One of the girls banged on the door. "Daddy!" Blessing hollered. "I'm hungry! I want a pink one!"

"Hold on," Evan said. "Let me get my socks." Even in the bathroom chilled by his cold shower, her perfume still lingered. Tabitha's ring twinkled beside the sink. Evan picked it up, reverentially running his thumb over the smooth white gold. Tears blurred the shape of the diamond. He'd bought it for her before they'd eloped to Australia. She'd been wearing an ocean blue skirt over a tiny white bikini, the diamond sparkling in the sunlight. Three carats of flawless marquise cut shining over Byron Bay as they said their vows. It fit perfectly.

She loved that ring. She'd loved him. For seven perfect years, she'd loved him.

The ring cut into his clenched fist. It hurt, but not as much as watching her walk out that door. The look in her eyes, disappointment and betrayal, hurt most of all.

What sort of idiot burns spaghetti sauce? *Oh, Tabitha, love. That isn't even the important question. What sort of idiot can't make his wife love him?*

Somehow he'd known all along she didn't really love him. Oh, there had been lust at first. An initial spark of interest that made everything the Morality Machine did possible. But he'd known in his heart-of-hearts that a woman like her could never love a man like him. He could have her body, but he could never have her admiration. Women like her wanted perfect men. Super men. Heroes, not villains.

It didn't matter.

He pulled on a clean shirt. Today he'd fix the Morality Machine, and tracking down Tabitha would be a simple matter of watching the news. He'd find her, turn on the machine, and fix this mess.

When Election Day rolled around, it wouldn't matter that he couldn't cook. He'd be president of the United States. If a computer geek who worked freelance out of his basement wasn't good enough for her, the president and de facto leader of the free world would be.

He pulled on his jacket out of habit and froze, captivated by his reflection in the mirror. The jacket, custom-tailored black Dior, had been off limits since the wedding. It always hung in the closet, a laughable reminder of life before her. The jacket radiated warmth, like a favorite blanket. It hugged him, promised him security.

"Daddy!" The scream at the door was accompanied by a ruckus that would make a zombie horde proud.

Toddlers and Dior didn't mix. The jacket went back in the closet. Today was a grease and gears day. The jacket could wait.

"You girls ready?" he asked with a big, fake smile as he opened the door.

CHAPTER TEN

I can count on one hand the number of times I have cried in my life. I cried when the doctors told us Blessing would live. I cried when we buried my parents after a drunk crossed the yellow line. Then Tabitha left me, and I learned what true sorrow was. There is no pain like losing the woman you love.

"MASTER?" HERT SIDLED up to the worktable cautiously.

Evan's gaze slid sideways to the paper Hert held, probably another calendar revision reminding him of the week he'd lost to the depression. "What?"

"We found her, Master." The minion held a paper out, quivering in terror.

"Give me that." Evan snatched it away. "I am not that scary," he shouted as Hert flinched.

The minions all ducked.

From across the room, Angela frowned at him from her throne of stuffed animals. He'd spent sleepless nights waiting for Tabitha to come home, clearing part of the lab and turning it into a kid-safe play area complete with ratty couch, old TV, and movies on VHS. The girls were fascinated by the ancient technology. Black ribbons of cassette tape hung from the ceiling like paper chains designed by Death.

He glowered back, and his daughter's eyes narrowed, making her look painfully like her mother.

A wave of happiness hit him. The gears spread out on the table looked like dancing daisies. Pink clouds floated past. Evan shook his head, but the pink clouds persisted. A small rainbow burst in front of him. "Angela?"

"Yes, Daddy?" she asked in a smug tone that was an exact replica of Tabby's when she'd just won a fight.

"Stop it, or you're grounded."

The pink clouds vanished, melting into the dungeon gray of the basement. His own dark feelings of self-hate and fear returned. "You should never manipulate people's emotions, Angela. That's what super villains do."

She unwound her blanket and walked over to his workbench. "Is that what you do?"

"What?" He looked up in alarm, then picked up a gear and made a show of studying it.

"You're a villain aren't you, Daddy?" He tapped the gear slowly on the tabletop.

"Of course not."

"Then why do you have machines and minions?"

Evan glanced at Hert. "They're cheaper than cats and dogs."

Angela crossed her arms. The other girls were paying attention now, cherubic faces peeking out of their blanket fort. "You make people agree with you."

"Obviously not," he growled, "or we wouldn't be having this argument."

"You're a super villain."

"Would your mother marry a super villain? She's a superhero. Everyone knows superheroes don't marry villains. There are rules."

Tears filled her eyes. "You tricked her! That's why she left us! You tricked her!"

"What? No! Sweetie, no." Evan scooped her up in a hug as guilt twisted in his gut like a knife. "No, Angela, no. Mommy knew I was a bad guy. I gave that up so I could be with her. I didn't trick her. I love her."

"But you are a villain," Angela said.

"Only as a hobby." He patted her back and rocked side to side like she was still three months old and easily calmed. He glanced at the paper Hert had pushed at him. "Girls? How would you like to go to Colorado?"

CHAPTER ELEVEN

Pick up and leave home? Home is where the heart is. Tabitha is the soul and center of my world. I could no more willingly live apart from her than I could will myself to quit breathing.

EVAN WATCHED FROM the foyer of the university biology building as students walked through the pine-studded campus. Tabitha stepped out of the library wearing jeans and a conservative t-shirt. His breath caught. She looked amazing. His heart raced as he waited for her to turn and smile. He needed that smile more than anything in the world.

"Mister Fascino?" The dean of the biology department opened his office door.

Evan tucked the cuff of his Dior suit shirtsleeve over the miniaturized Agree-With-Me Ray then turned with a smile. "Dean Lang, it's so good of you to see me at such short notice."

The giant of a man laughed heartily. "Trust me when I say, Mister Fascino, that I would rather speak with prospective teachers than the prospectus committee again. Drink?" he offered, motioning to a decanter of amber liquid sitting on a low side table near oversized windows.

"No, thank you." Evan took a seat and smiled at the dean. "I've found it's dangerous to accept unknown liquids from the biology department. Biologists have such a quirky sense of humor."

Dean Lang laughed. "We have more petri dishes filled with strawberry Jell-O on April Fools' Day than real specimens. That's eighteen-year-old Glenlivet whiskey, if you're interested. A gift from the family when I took the job." He settled his comfortable bulk into a dark leather chair. "So, you're interested in teaching here?"

"Yes, sir," Evan said, stepping away from mental calculations of how much the dean had spent on office furniture. "Professor Buckley mentioned there was an opening as an ethics lecturer. I've wanted an excuse to move to the area, so I thought I'd apply."

All of that was true. Since finding out that Tabitha had enrolled as a mid-semester transfer last week under the name Zinnia Perl, he was more than a little interested in moving to the foothills. Finding the aging Professor Buckley and persuading him to take an early retirement had taken all of ten minutes, in which time the professor had mentioned someone would need to fill his post as the ethics teacher—a class Tabitha took four days a week.

"And, have you ever taught ethics?" the dean asked.

"Not as such, sir. I hold dual degrees in genetics and mechanical engineering. I'm very familiar with the ethical quandaries of science. I've attended a number of ethics classes and symposiums." Mostly true. He'd tested out of a number of ethics classes, which was practically the same thing.

Evan adjusted the mini Agree-With-Me Ray clipped to his watch. "Why don't I start today?"

The dean blinked at him with an expression of bovine confusion.

Being in that class was essential to life. If he couldn't see Tabitha soon he wouldn't survive another day. He needed something from her, a look, a gesture, something to give him hope.

She'd have no way to ignore him. Angry as she was, she wouldn't miss the chance to ask about the girls. Maybe threaten him.

It didn't matter. She could break every bone in his body if it meant she'd consider forgiving him. He tapped the watch again. "Class starts in a few minutes. You want me there."

"Ah," said the dean, shaking his head. "Are you... Are you quite ready to teach? I could have someone else fill in."

"No need. Professor Buckley was kind enough to give me a copy of his lecture notes. I know the material."

Dean Lang rubbed his temples. "Well, if you're quite sure. I suppose I could, um... Ah."

"Write up my packet and finish the paperwork," Evan suggested. "That would be perfect. I'll come by and sign everything tomorrow."

"Right." He shuffled paper. "I'm sorry, did you already send your credentials over? I don't recall seeing them."

"I'm sure you saw them. You complimented me on the thesis paper I wrote." Evan arched an eyebrow. *Stubborn old man. Agree-With-Me!*

"Quite. Yes, of course I remember now. Age and all." The dean gave him a weak smile.

Evan stood up. "Thank you so much for the job, Dean. I look forward to working here."

He ran to the classroom, a small lecture hall on the far side of campus, featuring orange plastic chairs and fake wooden desktops. He scanned the crowd, but couldn't find Tabitha.

Taking a deep breath, he walked down to the teaching podium and pretended to busy himself with the papers. The material wasn't all that interesting, only a review of free market eugenics and the synthetic life form *Mycoplasma mycoidesJCVI-syn1.0*.

The classroom door opened, bringing the smell of dying leaves and something a little too sweet for pleasure. Tabitha's new perfume.

He looked up, drinking the sight of her in as he tried to prepare an argument for the coming confrontation. He wasn't following her; he was here for the job. She'd said something about finding work, hadn't she?

Tabitha took her seat, glanced at him with an easy smile, and then looked away as if he were the least important thing in the world. Again.

Somehow, Evan managed to stumble through the fifty-minute class without begging Tabitha's forgiveness.

Her sweet smile dominated his thoughts as he rambled on about medical testing and... something. There were words, he strung them in sentences, none of that mattered. He felt fifteen again, lost in a hell of shame and fear. Finally, the lecture ended and he could say, "Time's up. Make sure to study chapter twelve for the quiz on Friday."

The students filed out. Tabitha collected her books as she chatted with a friend, then turned to look at him with a pretty, pink blush on her cheeks.

He licked his lips as she walked down the aisle between long rows of stadium seats. A wiser man might have run, but he couldn't. He'd do anything to see her again, take any abuse just to be near her.

She trapped him with her smile as surely as any cage. "Doctor?" she asked, an innocent note of hesitancy in her voice.

"Mister Fascino, for now." He smiled. "I'm still waiting to defend my thesis." Wrong answer. He cleared his throat. "Evan works best." *Or Love, Lover, Sexy, Husband, any of those.* It didn't matter what she called him. If she spoke, he would listen.

"Evan." Her mouth curled around his name the way it did in bed when she begged for release. A prayer, a charm, a promise—on her lips his name became a many-faceted thing. "Are you coming to the department mixer tonight?" she asked.

"Um, what?" He'd been lost in memory.

"The mixer. It's not quite a dinner, but they usually have pizza and punch, store-bought cookies. You know the drill. We all come and socialize."

"You like pizza?"

"Love it!" She laughed, the way she always did when they were alone together, and happy.

What was that supposed to mean? There was no hand signal, no hint of what she was thinking. Just Tabitha clutching her books to her chest and looking virginal as the day they married. "Um, I don't know. I wasn't planning on going."

"You should come," she said. "We graduate students have to stick together."

"Right."

Her hand reached for his, a butterfly's touch. "I'd like you to come."

If she'd asked him for the moon, he would have found a way to put it in her hands by supper. "I'll be there."

She walked away. No backward glance. No significant eye gesture to signal she'd left a note.

Nothing.

Evan checked under her desk, under his desk, and by the door. Not even a pencil shaving.

It didn't make sense. She stormed out of the house furious, and now she acted like she couldn't wait to see him at dinner? Dinner? Was there some sort of coded message? A cryptogram spelled out in pepperoni?

There had to be a rational explanation for all of this.

He fiddled with his watch and froze. The Agree-With-Me Ray? It wasn't supposed to work like that. He should have been able to persuade her to listen, but it wasn't the Morality Machine. Not by a long shot. If it worked like that, everyone from Dean Lang to Tabby's new BFF would be offering to show him their private leather-and-lace collection.

He grabbed his phone and dialed. "Hert?"

"Yes, Master?"

"How are the girls?"

"Watching a movie, Master. There is popcorn everywhere."

"Fine. Did you get the video feed of Tabby?"

"Yes."

"And? What was the signal? What did she do? Did she do something at super speed I didn't see?"

"We're still analyzing, Master, but I don't believe she did anything except invite you to dinner."

Evan chewed his lip for a minute. "All right. New plan. Find out where this mixer is, get a team in to bug her apartment, and pick some minions to watch the girls. It looks like I'm going to have a late night."

CHAPTER TWELVE

There should be some background story about my awkward youth or how I was teased as a child, or even how my parents never loved me. I could write that story, but it would all be lies. No one pushed me into a life of crime. I've never tried to excuse my behavior that way. I've never tried to excuse my behavior at all.

As a boy, I was precocious. As a teen, I was handsome. I never wanted for attention or adoration, but I always wanted more. Intelligent people often take up challenging hobbies to pass the time. I took up the idea of world domination and, unlike all the Goth aficionados in black lipstick, I didn't sit around paying lip service to the idea. I chased my dreams until the day my dreams changed.

That happens sometimes. Even the best plans need reconsideration when a better offer comes along. When my choice came down to having the world or having Tabitha, I wanted her more.

EVAN SCROUNGED AROUND the makeshift lab in the rented house. The small, four-bedroom brick Tudor near the university wasn't much, the only real selling points were the partial basement for his lab and the fenced yard for the girls.

While his minions were still busy trying to unpack all the toys, he worked like a maniac on the Morality Machine. "Hert, did we find that part?"

"The crystal focus, Master? Yes, we have one left."

"Only one? I need a second one for redundant back up. Using only one focus was my mistake the first time."

The minion shuffled his webbed feet.

"What?"

"The other is in the Election Ray, sir. I would have to cannibalize that—"

"Never mind." Evan turned back to the Morality Machine with a glare. "It'll work. Start running the tests so we can get this calibrated. I need to go get dressed."

Hert frowned at him as he hurried upstairs. Evan pointedly ignored the look. There were hundreds of things he needed to be doing this week. Chasing down Tabitha hadn't been on the agenda, but he couldn't put it off another day, not even another hour.

"Daddy?" Angela walked over to him clutching her stuffed dog. "Where is Mommy?"

"You said Mommy would be here," Blessing re-minded him.

Maria and Delilah joined their sisters. Four pairs of eyes watched him with innocent expressions of hope.

Time to lie. "Mommy is working undercover to stop something bad. I'm going to go meet with her tonight, and find out how long this project will take."

"I want to see Mommy," Delilah said.

"And I promise, Mommy wants to see you. Maybe she can sneak out to see us tomorrow." He made a mental note to arrange that. "I'm going to get changed real quick, okay? Are you girls all sett-led in? Do you like your new rooms?" They nodded. He settled them in the living room where they could watch a movie with Hert and the other min-ions could guard them.

Tabitha wanted to see him. That put it all in per-spective. She'd come to talk to him.

Obviously, there was a plan. He'd go to the mixer and get a clue. Who knew, maybe he hadn't lied about her being undercover. Maybe the whole mess the other morning had been an act.

Evan made a mental note to have the minions check for bugs and began pulling clothes from a hastily packed box. He didn't know what to wear. A classy tux? No. Mixer. What did people wear to mixers? He pulled some faded jeans and a white t-shirt from the box. He hated the generic, blue-collar look, but Tabby loved it. Something about a man in jeans worked for her, and never failed to get him laid. He needed a 'No Fail' plan just now.

The mixer was held in the biology department building's main lecture hall. The maintenance staff had cleared away the chairs. Sad crepe-paper flowers in school colors lay amid the greasy pizza boxes like the tattered standards of a lost legion.

Evan tugged needlessly at his shirt, turned his mini Agree-With-Me Ray to full, and stepped into the room with a confident smile. He'd been to parties before; this wasn't one. On the scale of entertainment, it ranked somewhere between filing taxes—something he never did—and attending a birthday party with clowns and thirty crying toddlers.

Finding Tabitha was a matter of finding the largest crowd of stuttering males. They surrounded her like Neanderthals worshiping a sun goddess.

Across the semi-crowded room, their eyes met. Blue eyes sparkled like sunlight on the waves. He'd never get tired of that come-hither look.

Evan raised an eyebrow, a silent commentary on her crowd of admirers, and walked to the buffet table to score a cookie. Doctor Charm's arsenal included flirting. Running to her would only rank him alongside the rest of her adoring sycophants. Husband or not, he had to follow the rules of the game.

When she was ready, she'd break free.

And she did. Evan nearly spit punch all over the white linoleum when he saw her walking toward him with an easy smile on her face. She didn't look angry. One corner of his mouth lifted in a half smile. That body... All those curves, the satin-soft skin... He was in lust all over again.

"You broke away from the crowd," he said, sipping his drink to keep from claiming her lips. The memory of her taste turned the sweet punch sour. "Is it always so lively?"

Tabitha shrugged, blushing. "We're a department of people watchers."

"Maybe we should hire someone to party while we watch." He kept her gaze.

Tabitha licked her lips. He almost bent down to chase her tongue and coax it out to play. She giggled, a sweet sound that promised beautiful things.

Maybe he needed to find a dark corner and see if she was interested in a fast anatomy lesson. No. Focus. Wife. "So..." Evan cast around for a topic. "Are you here with anyone?"

Why are we here? was an even better question, but she'd told him to be here, so the answer to everything was here. *Give me a hint, Tabby-cat.*

"Oh." She tucked a loose strand of hair behind her ear. "I'm just here with my roommate, Hilary. There's..." She giggled again and looked at the floor. "There's no one." Blue eyes looked up at him. "Are you seeing anyone?"

Evan took a breath. Deep cover was not a comfortable place to be. Swirling the punch around his cup, he shrugged. "It's complicated."

"How can it be complicated? You're either with someone or you aren't." Her hands went to her hips, the flirt was gone. "So, status?"

"It depends."

"On what?"

"Do you love me?"

She blinked, caught off guard.

"Zinnia! Zinnia, there you are." A blond man built like a rugby player cut between them. He looked vaguely familiar. "There you are, Zee-girl. Sorry I'm late." He gave Evan a passing glance. "Who's your friend?"

"Evan Fascino, the new ethics professor."

"Ethics professor?" Rugby laughed. "You ever get laid, or are you, like, the fifty-year-old virgin?" He grabbed Tabitha's arm and she winced.

"Are you all right?" Evan asked Tabitha, blocking Rugby with an upheld arm.

Tabitha looked confused. "I'm fine. I hurt my arm falling down some stairs."

"Stairs?" The fight. He hadn't even asked her about the fight. "Let me see."

"Dude, I got it." Rugby pushed him back. "I do sports medicine."

More likely he did anything too drunk to object.

Rugby pulled out an alcohol wipe, rolled Tabitha's sleeve up, and peeled back the bandage. An angry red gash ran parallel to the scar he'd given her.

Evan felt his heart skip a beat. This was all his fault. And now some chump was pawing his wife. "Can I help?"

"No, I got it," Rugby said, waving the wipe past Evan's nose. A sharp, super sweet smell assailed him.

Evan sneezed. "What is that?"

"This? Just a homeopathic recipe my grandma used to use, mostly lotus blossom. Way better than alcohol. Doesn't smell bad either. Right, Zee?" He shoved the wipe toward Tabitha's face.

She grimaced and turned her head. "Better than alcohol, I guess."

"Thane!" someone shouted from the other side of the room.

Rugby frowned. "Be right back. Zee, you wait."

"I'll wait for you," Tabitha said as her smile faded. When she turned back to Evan her expression was vague, disinterested.

"So, that's your boyfriend?" Evan felt himself losing his grip on reality as the storm of emotions swept him away. His wife. His. *Wife!* And she let some strange man patch her up. "Is he why you're here?"

"What? I'm here because he asked me to wait." Her face filled with confusion. She rubbed her temples. "I'm sorry. Sometimes I get these headaches. What were you asking?"

Evan unclenched his jaw to say, "I was asking if you and Rugby were an item."

"Thane and I?" She shook her head. "He's like that with everyone. He's a super... a super protective person." Her eyes lost focus again. "He wants what's best for everyone."

"And that means bossing you around?" The temperature of the conversation continued to plummet.

"I'm here alone. My parents live in Wisconsin. I'm not a city girl. I feel out of place here. Thane's a real friend."

Evan stared at her. "Wisconsin?" Tabitha's parents owned a condo in Miami. She'd grown up in West Palm. So why did Wisconsin sound so familiar? He stepped back, not sure what was happening anymore.

"Evan?" Tabitha touched his arm lightly. He raised an eyebrow, not sure how to go on. "Have you ever met someone that you trust implicitly from the first time you see them?" She sounded so hesitant. Fearful.

"A few," he admitted grudgingly, letting her soft touch reel him back in.

A warm smile brought life back to her green eyes. "I feel like that with you. I don't believe in past lives or anything, but I feel like I know you." She squeezed his arm. "I'm so glad you're here. We're going to be great friends."

He stared at her. *'I don't even know you,'* she'd said as she walked out on him. The words reverberated through his head. Gently, he lifted her hand to his lips. "You can trust me. With everything."

"Ready to fly, Zee?" Rugby Thane butted back in. "We've got kicking dinner plans."

Tabitha turned to Thane, the smile falling from her face. "Sounds great."

CHAPTER THIRTEEN

I should probably say a word about my competition. There is none. As far as you and the rest of the world is concerned, I am the pinnacle of creation, and I have a machine that will make you nod your head in agreement as I say that.

There are other super villains, of course. They tend to crop up like mushrooms in the wake of every major disaster. I consider them useful. They keep the superheroes occupied and out of my hair while I take over the world. Some of them are even good enough to become reoccurring headlines. But they aren't as good as me.

Seeing Tabitha with another man, seeing her smile and leave with another man, was a punch to the gut. I'd give up major limbs before I let another man have my wife, but what could I do? She acted like she didn't know me. Like seven years of marriage never happened. I couldn't compete with that.

If Tabitha wanted me, I'd fight to the death for her. But when she walked away of her own free will, I was lost.

EVAN STRODE OUT of the building, ready to kill someone for the first time in his life. She didn't know him.

She didn't know him, and she was going to dinner with another man.

He dialed the lab. "Hert, I need perfume samples. Lots of them. And I need the Morality Machine dismantled now. Now! There's something wrong here. What? What girls?"

His girls. He was already going to hell for not belonging to any of the right religions, stealing money, and being a super villain. Compared to that, forgetting his daughters for a few minutes while his life fell apart was... He took a deep breath. Unforgivable. No wonder Tabitha didn't love him.

Rubbing his wrist, he took the mini Agree-With-Me Ray off. It hadn't worked. Maybe it even hurt her. He sucked in the pine-scented night air and tried to focus.

Evan could think of two possible explanations why Tabitha didn't remember him. The first, and the most obvious, was that the Morality Machine had affected her memory and personality more than he'd anticipated. She still seemed attracted to him, so had he been breaking down her memories all this time, rather than her morals?

The other option was that something else had stolen her memories. A head injury in the fight? She hadn't hit her head on the ground, but maybe she had a concussion from the creature hitting her?

Or she was so angry with him she'd blocked him out of her memory? Or... He dug through his mental file of possibilities.

The smell of Thane's homeopathic treatment bothered him. Maybe because her shirts reeked of it when she came home from the fight. Evan looked up at the cold starlight. The smell, the t-shirts, and a tall blond man.

He'd never paid much attention to superheroes and their identities. Some villains dedicated years to researching a nemesis. A few went as far as fixating on superheroes, but that was too creepy-stalker-freak for him.

Superheroes came, and after a polite chat, they went away. Except Tabitha. He'd been too spellbound to speak before she broke the Agree-With-Me Ray.

But the big, blond Thane, he looked... Evan slapped his thigh. Time for the professor to do a little homework.

At home, Evan pulled out all the reference material he'd amassed on superheroes, super villains, and the unsolved crimes of the last century. Most of it he'd stolen, some of it had been compiled from court records and newspaper printouts by the minions, and none of it was alphabetized.

Blessing snuggled on his lap as he paged through the reports on superheroes unmasked. Delilah and Maria helped the minions sort the Morality Machine parts, and Angela thumbed through a thick book.

"Here we go," Evan said, shifting Blessing to his knee. "The Rainbow Dane, also known as Thane Mitely, raised by a single mother named Ava Mitely. It's rumored that his father was the Roaring Thane, and that's where his name came from." He set the papers down, frowning. "I don't remember the Roaring Thane."

Hert tilted his head. "I've read about him, sir. He was one of the early superheroes. Super strength, if I recall correctly."

"Who did he fight?"

"Everyone, sir. He fought any and all crime. If he saw a wrongdoing he'd roar, hence the name, and attack."

"So, what, drug dealers and hippies? Corrupt cops? What was his MO?"

"Anything, sir. Jaywalkers, clerks giving wrong change, people who ran stoplights. He said once that he could tell someone was going to commit a crime before they acted."

Evan shook his head. "Sounds psycho to me."

"The police objected as well, but he helped enough that they were hesitant to stop him. He was killed in a fight with the Magenta Fox, who in turn was killed by the Roaring Thane's mother. She called herself Lady Grimoire and her super skill, if you call it that, was potions."

"Interesting."

"When the superheroes first appeared in the public they weren't under any code of conduct with the government. The only thing separating a villain from a hero was media perception," Hert said.

"I can't say the registration card scheme has changed that." Evan drummed his fingers on the floor.

"Daddy?" Blessing asked. "What does this say?" She pointed to a caption under a black and white photo of a little girl on a swing in front of pine trees.

"Zinnia Perl, age four, near her childhood home of—" Evan gasped, taking the book away from Blessing. "I'd forgotten all about this. It's in her book, the one we wrote the year she was pregnant. Some news reporter kept calling to demand the official story of her life, so she finally wrote the autobiography just to keep people from asking questions. It was her tell-all book!"

"Daddy?" Blessing pulled the book back. "Is this Mommy?"

"Yes. Her parents took her to Aspen for Christmas that year. It was a generic snow picture." He had sorted hundreds of old photos trying to find the ones that didn't have enough detail to unravel her false history. Evan snapped his fingers. "Hert, listen. I have two theories."

"Very good, Master."

"The first is that the Morality Machine breaking somehow caused Tabitha to lose her memory of everything that's happened since I turned it on."

"A possibility, Master. Although an unlikely one."

"Right. The Morality Machine shouldn't show precise brain damage like that. Maybe it would affect impulse control, but not memory. My second theory is that someone has taken, or suppressed, her memory."

His minion frowned. "I haven't heard of anyone working on memory, sir."

Evan sighed. "Yes, that's where it falls apart."

Angela walked over and sat in his lap. "When do we get to see Mommy?"

He studied the girls for a minute. "How does tomorrow sound?"

Their eyes lit up. "Really? Tomorrow? Promise?" The cacophony of four piping voices drowned out his reply for a good minute.

Evan waited it out. When they finally fell silent, he smiled grimly. "Daddy needs more data so he can prove his theory. Do you want to be my ice cream minions tomorrow?"

Maria raised an eyebrow in an exact copy of his favorite cynical pose. "What's an ice cream minion?"

"It means I pay you in ice cream cones to help me follow Mommy." The clapping started. "One ice cream cone per person. Not multiple cones per kid," he clarified.

The clapping stuttered away.

"Go upstairs and get pajamas on. Tomorrow we are stalking a superhero!"

He waited for them to go upstairs before turning to Hert. "Find out Tabitha's schedule for tomorrow. It's a Saturday. Maybe see if you can lure her to a park or something. I think that once she sees the girls, she'll remember them at least. No woman forgets her children after twenty hours of labor. If this is some joke she's playing on me because she's angry..."

He took a deep breath to steady himself. "She won't pretend that she doesn't know the girls. It doesn't matter how angry she is with me. She wouldn't hurt them."

CHAPTER FOURTEEN

I can only recall one instance before this where I truly felt nervous: the night I waited to see Tabitha the second time.

Expectation was pure torture. Every breeze that brushed past the warehouse door made me turn. Every noise made me jump. I'd put everything into this one gamble, wagered everything on getting my machine right the first time.

In retrospect, I could have tried the Morality Machine on any number of victims. But at the time, it never occurred to me. My entire focus was on winning Zephyr Girl for myself.

When she arrived, words failed me. She was beautiful. Beyond beautiful. She put Helen and her thousand ships to shame. She made springtime seem dowdy, and long summer days plain. Zephyr Girl landed lightly and sauntered toward me, an unfathomable expression on her face. "Hello, Doctor Charm. Or should I say Evan?"

I hesitated, holding the control for the Morality Machine and drinking in her beauty. "I knew you wouldn't stay away."

She laughed, the sound of angels. "Do you know why I'm here?"

I looked away then, wishing the burning kiss she'd left me with would lead to more without mechanical intervention and knowing it wouldn't. "I can guess." And just like that, I flipped the switch that changed her life.

When I looked up, her eyes had filled with erotic hunger. "I want you. Against the wall. On the table. I want a blistering hot love affair that will keep the tabloids talking for decades."

"Really?" Vivid images filled my mind. I'd never brought a girl home to the lab before her, but it was years before I could look at some of my machines without picturing her stretched over them wearing nothing but her thigh-high boots.

I remember, now, that I fumbled for the ring. It was the first time in my life I felt truly sinister. I was taking something I knew no woman as beautiful as Tabitha would ever offer me.

My hand shook as I held the ring box out. "Why don't you marry me instead?"

She froze, and I swallowed a curse, certain the Morality Machine wasn't strong enough.

And then she was wrapped around me. Fingers tangled in my hair, her lips teasing mine. Torso... Well, a gentleman doesn't divulge all the details. Suffice it to say, I thought my conquest was complete.

CHASING FOUR STICKY children around a strange city on an unbelievably warm October day counted as a torture more cruel than even the most depraved super villain could devise. Pitchforks and eternal damnation had nothing on whiny, tired children who just wanted their mother. Evan collapsed into a park bench as the girls tore into their third ice cream cone each.

Delilah looked up at him with a huge smile ringed in blue. "I love you, Daddy!"

"Love you too, pumpkin."

"Can we have cookies when we get home?"

He raised an eyebrow at her. "I thought you girls weren't going to give Daddy a heart attack until you turned sixteen and started driving. All this sugar is killing me."

Delilah frowned at him. "I don't remember that."

"I remember it distinctly. Right after you were born you signed a contract."

Her eyes narrowed and she turned to her sisters. "Did we sign a contract with Daddy?"

"In sparkly purple pen," Evan added. "I distinctly remember the ink was sparkly purple."

The girls fell into earnest discussion, giving him a moment to breathe. Across the park, something caught his eye. A familiar silhouette in the afternoon sun. Tabitha.

Blessing gasped. "Mommy!"

"Wait!" Evan caught her arm before disaster

struck. "Mommy is undercover, remember?"

"Ooooo." Four innocent, ice cream-smeared faces turned to him.

"We're going to go play catch, and Mommy is going to give us a sign. But you have to pretend you don't know her. Okay? We don't want the bad guys to find out about Mommy." He looked each of the girls in the eye. "Do you understand?"

"Yes, Daddy," they chorused.

"Good." He watched Tabitha for a moment, heart in his throat. This was the only way to know. Even if she was angry with him, Tabitha wouldn't ignore the girls. If the Morality Machine had erased her memory... Well, that was a bridge he would burn later. "Come on, girls, let's go play catch."

They played with an over-sized pink softball. Delilah tossed it to Angela, Angela tossed the ball to Maria, and Maria tossed to Blessing, who tossed it to Evan.

Tabitha sat down in the grass, talking animatedly with her friend while she flipped open a psychology textbook.

A few more times around the circle and Evan growled in frustration. "New plan!" he told the girls. "Let's make teams. Blessing and Maria against Delilah and Angela."

"Whose team are you on, Daddy?" Angela asked.

"I'm going to be the monkey in the middle. If I catch the ball I get to throw it anywhere in the park."

Delilah put her hands on her hips. "Anywhere?"

"Anywhere. Even up a tree!"

"Not fair!" Maria protested.

Evan shrugged. "I suppose you better keep the ball away from me then."

They threw the ball around him, rolled it between his feet, and once Angela threw it so hard he had to duck or risk a serious head injury. All the while, Tabitha talked blithely on as if her four beautiful daughters weren't mere feet away.

Desperate for some sign, Evan jumped after the ball. He grabbed it, twisted away, and rolled the softball so it bumped against Tabitha's foot.

She looked down at the pink ball in surprise, then smiled brightly as Blessing went running up. "Is this your ball?"

Blessing stared, and finally nodded. "Uh huh. Daddy bought it for me."

"What a nice Daddy you have," Tabitha said. She handed the ball to Blessing. "Here you go."

Blessing moped back to the circle. She looked back at Tabitha. "Daddy, why didn't Mommy say she loves me? She always says she loves me."

Tears and fear choked him.

"She's undercover!" Angela said in exasperation. "Weren't you listening?"

Blessing nodded. "I forgot. I thought she was going to wink at me."

Evan struggled to find his voice. "Undercover agents don't wink," he lied.

They played ball for a few more minutes, but the girls had lost interest. They wanted their mommy. The one that didn't recognize them anymore, thanks to him. Eventually, Evan caught the ball and steered them away from the park.

Back at the rental house, he served a dinner of ramen noodles and grape juice. Everything reeked of failure. He read the girls their bedtime story, tucked them in, and slunk off to the improvised lab.

Hert looked up as he entered. "Good evening, Master. I have excellent news."

Evan raised an eyebrow as he collapsed onto an up-turned crate.

"The latest Election Ray results are very promising. I believe we have the calibration 95 percent perfected."

He nodded wearily.

"Sir?" The minion looked confused. "Isn't that good news?"

"What about the Morality Machine, Hert? Where do we stand with that?"

"Um." The warty minion checked his clipboard. "Not finished, sir. We've inspected all the components and run all the tests you specified. There is nothing conclusive."

Evan covered his eyes, aware that he was too exhausted to move, but unwilling to give up. Failure wasn't something he could accept. There had to be a way to fix this.

Hert cleared his throat. "If I may say, sir, it would help immensely if you were in the lab during the day."

"I can't be in the lab! The girls need me!"

Hert gave him a flat stare. "Sir, I am genetically programmed to point out personal inconsistencies that hinder your work. Sir, you did nothing today."

"I took the girls to see Tabitha."

"No, sir. You walked around the city eating unhealthy amounts of frozen non-dairy concoctions mooning for a woman who left you."

Evan surged to his feet. "She didn't leave me. Tabitha wouldn't leave me. She wouldn't leave the girls. She... forgot who we are."

Hert cleared his throat again. "Sir? The Morality Machine doesn't work that way. I can think of no way the Morality Machine could affect a person's memory. The magnetic waves specifically target the posterior pituitary gland to excite production of vasopressin."

"She's a superhero. No one really knows how their body chemistry works. It's a mix up. It's just... Just..." He paced in the tiny rat-trap of a basement. Swallowing back a lump in his throat, Evan took a deep breath. "I need some fresh air. I need to think. Watch the girls."

He walked out of the garage, not quite sure where he was headed. While his mind swirled with all the possibilities and implications, he found himself walking under the looming shadow of the university library.

A few late lights dotted the campus buildings. The students were off partying, or sleeping, or visiting family. Anything but studying, if he remembered college correctly.

A chill wind stirred the pine trees, bringing the first scent of winter. How had it all gone so wrong?

He had a timetable. He was supposed to be a few days away from the single greatest achievement any American could have. The world should be unfolding at his feet. Nothing on the timetable mentioned Tabitha storming out, or—the word he'd danced around—divorce.

With a sigh, he collapsed onto a bench, staring into the darkness as he waited for an answer.

CHAPTER FIFTEEN

I can't recall a time I truly felt guilty. Even when one of my minions ate all of Great-Grandmother's fine china my senior year of high school. Guilt was the same thing as getting in trouble, and I could always talk my way out of trouble.

The only person with any measure of control over my actions was myself. I think that's true of everyone, although most people will deny it. There is no angel or devil sitting on your shoulder telling you what to do. Laws are there as pleasant reminders of the consequences that await the foolish, but in the end the only authority a person can rely on is their own.

And you know what? You can't sweet talk yourself. There was no rationalization for what I had done. Not a single thing I could say that made the situation better. I had the perfect life, and I'd lost it being stupid.

I could bend the will of anyone I met to suit my needs, but I could never force them to give me the one thing I always craved.

Even with the Morality Machine, I couldn't force someone to love me. I tricked Tabitha into love, but the emotion was tainted. Seven years of lust with never a moment of true love. It was the one-night stand that never ended, until the machine broke and Tabitha walked back to her life with nary a backward glance.

WIND RUSTLED THROUGH the pine trees, bringing the scent of wood smoke and car fumes. Evan sat back in the park bench with a sigh, watching the sun sink low over the mountains as he replayed the afternoon's encounter in his mind.

This wasn't the end. He wouldn't let it be the end. Somehow he could find a way to get Tabitha back. If he couldn't, what was the point of going on?

The girls, obviously. They needed a parent, although a stuffed zucchini would probably do a better job than he was at this point.

Tabitha's laugh broke through his misery.

He looked around and spotted her walking into a large, square building across from the park. He ran to catch the door as it swung closed and stepped into what looked like an unused gymnastics center, complete with a sad pair of rings hanging off to one side over a cracked mat. He could smell the faded sweat from glory days long past.

A large woman in tight blue spandex walked past, completely ignoring him.

The door shut quietly behind him as he took in the rainbow array of spandex suits. Apparently Tabitha had joined an aerobics class for the middle-aged and balding. One violently yellow suit with red zigzags on the far side of the gym caught his attention—The Rolling Shock.

Evan looked around, trying to find other familiar faces.

When he knew what to look for he could see the old gymnasium was packed with the full roster of superheroes he'd defeated. He stepped into the shadows, weighing his options. The Rainbow Dane was there, standing on the far side under a spotlight in earnest discussion with Hempman and The Rolling Shock. All three a good reason to leave. But Tabitha was there too, still dressed in her jeans and t-shirt, and holding court with Angler Girl, The Buxom Boss, and The Starlit Starlet near a table of snacks.

Had Tabitha left him for this? He'd been searching for the complicated answer, but what if the simple one had been right all along? What if all she wanted was to be with her own kind? Evan watched her as he leaned back against the door, casually preventing any more heroes from joining the party.

Tabitha had bags under her eyes, and her gestures were agitated. At a glance, she looked like a woman under extreme stress. He'd never seen her miserable before—one point in his favor despite everything—and now that he knew what it might look like, he knew he'd never be able to bear the real thing. Starlit grabbed a cookie and noticed him, his buttoned down shirt and slacks didn't help him blend into the crowd. Starlit straightened, preening and smiling in an inviting way that would have worked if he were still sixteen, single, and had never seen Zephyr Girl. Really, the other superheroes should have kicked Tabitha out years ago for being too beautiful for their collective good.

Starlit said something, and the other women turned. Tabitha's eyes widened. She excused herself from the others, and made a beeline for his position by the door.

"Professor," she hissed, grabbing his arm. "What are you doing here?"

"I was taking a walk when I saw you come inside. Is this another department shindig?"

Gore Smasher walked past and Evan stopped to stare at the layer of flab jiggling in purple spandex. "Was I supposed to wear a costume? Halloween isn't until tomorrow, but I'm game." Bemused and befuddled professor was as good a cover as any.

"No. This is a private party." Tabitha was pushing him to the door. "Professor, please, you need to leave."

He caught her hand, warm and soft. Evan couldn't look her in the eyes. If he did, he'd be lost. He'd fall right there, kiss her, steal her away. "You don't look like you're dressed for this party either. Why not come with me? We can grab a late snack."

"I... I can't." She tugged at her hair nervously. "I'm sort of..." She rolled her eyes. "I'm playing hostess. My friends really feel strongly about this, and we're trying to get more people involved."

"Oh, so this is a political thing?" Evan kept the anger in check.

Tabitha snuck a look over her shoulder at the Rainbow Dane. "Sort of. It's almost political."

Starlit did a wiggly finger wave and motioned for him to join them.

Evan hit the small Agree-With-Me Ray on his arm. "Look the other way," he said, just loud enough for it to carry.

As everyone else turned away, Tabitha turned back to him. "You really don't belong here."

"The question is, do you belong here?" He squeezed her hand. "You don't look happy. To me, that's a good indicator that you don't want to be here. So why not leave?"

"I can't!" Finally she looked at him, blue eyes blazing. "I can't leave. We have a deadline. This is important. Our group is trying to stop villains. Super villains."

"And?" Evan asked with deceptive casualness.

"Some of us want to aim for the younger vill-ains." The color drained from her face. "They want to stop them before they can hurt anyone."

A cold chill ran up his spine. "There's a lot of wiggle room in that statement. How young are your friends thinking of aiming?"

Tears glistened in Tabitha's eyes. "As soon as we can find them. A child of a superhero becomes a superhero. A child of super villain..." She choked.

Evan pulled her into his arms as she started to cry. "You don't want to do this, do you?" he whispered in her ear. Against his shirt, she shook her head. Hot tears melted through the fabric. "Shhh, it's okay. You don't have to do this."

Tabitha pulled away. "I have to make the world safe. I have to stop villains before they hurt anyone. It's who I am. I... I don't have a choice. We start tomorrow. The Rainbow Dane says we can't wait any longer."

"Correct me if I'm wrong, but a person can't be a villain until they do something wrong. Innocent until proven guilty and all that."

Tabitha shook her head. "That's not what—"

"Who in the blue blazes are you?" The Rainbow Dane roared grabbing Tabitha's arm and pulling her away. "Zephyr, get over here. Who is this schmuck?"

"He's... he's my ethics professor." Tabitha wiped away a tear.

"Shock!" the Dane shouted. "Get Zee a drink, she's not feeling like herself."

"I'm fine!" Tabitha protested. She tried to step away, but The Rolling Shock grabbed her, stunning her still and forcing a drink to her lips.

Evan knocked it out of his hands. "The lady said she wasn't thirsty."

The collected superheroes stared at him as if he was a fuzzy bunny that had suddenly turned into a carnivore.

"I don't know what sort of games you're playing," Evan said. "I see the costumes, and I don't know the rules, but I do know that when a lady says no, she means no. Now, let Miss Perl go."

The Rainbow Dane chuckled. His laugh rolled like thunder, and soon the whole room joined in. "Oh, Pops, we ain't at the university anymore. This is real life, and around here, we don't play games. Shock, show the nutty professor here the door."

The Rolling Shock grinned maliciously as he strutted toward Evan.

Evan pressed the Agree-With-Me Ray just in time. "I'm not here. Nothing happened."

The Rolling Shock froze mid-step. The entire party turned, acting as if nothing had happened.

Evan rushed back to Tabitha. "Sweetheart, can you hear me?" The sickly sweet smell that had clung to her since the fight assaulted him. He picked up the cup she'd dropped. Not perfume, but this. The same smell as the homeopathic lotus wash the Thane had wiped her cut with.

Cut. Blood. Drug. Blood stream.

Gingerly holding the edges of the cup, Evan wrapped it in a napkin and tucked it in his pocket. "Hold on, Tabby-cat. I'll be back for you."

CHAPTER SIXTEEN

What is the difference between a villain and a hero? I never thought to ask. As I walked away from Tabitha that night, I knew one thing: even if she never loved me, I was going to save her. Tabitha was trapped. My children were threatened. This meant war.

EVAN TUGGED AT the cuffs of his tuxedo. "Hert? How do I look?"

"Charming as ever, Doctor." The minion ran a rag over the toe of his shoe. "There, sir. Quite ready to take over the world."

"That plan is on hold," Evan said as he glided into the garage.

An owl cried mournfully in the distance as the minions stilled to look at him. "On hold, sir?"

He hit the assembly with the megawatt smile he hadn't used in years. "I've declared war on the superheroes."

A purple minion with a yellow Mohawk fell backward in a faint.

Hert clicked his tongue. "War, sir? Alone? Against how many superheroes?"

"All of them. Except Tabitha, of course."

"Of course." Hert set down his clipboard with delicate care. "Sir, are you quite sure you're feeling well?"

He tossed the cup to Hert. "That's what they're using to poison Tabitha. I think it's a derivative of the lotus flower, but double check anyway. I want an antidote by morning. The Rainbow Dane stole my wife and he wants to kill my daughters because they are the children of a super villain." Evan's eye twitched just a little. "He will not have that opportunity."

"Understood, sir." Hert clutched his clipboard again like a long lost teddy bear. "I think I can find other super villains, if we have a few days time."

"We don't have days. I'm going in alone—"

"Daddy?" a sleepy voice asked from the doorway.

"Angela? Why aren't you in bed, sweetie?"

She rubbed sleepy eyes. "You were being loud. Is Mommy home yet?"

"Um." He bit his lip as he scrambled for a plausible lie.

Angela looked at his Dior suit. "Where are you going, Daddy?"

"To deal with a very bad man, Angel."

"Are you going to hurt him?"

"That's a possibility."

She yawned. "Can I come?"

Evan's eye twitched again. "No, sweetie. You are going to stay here where it's nice and safe." In his mind, a vivid image of the Rainbow Dane attacking the girls while he rushed to rescue Tabitha bloomed in Technicolor. The minions would do their best to keep the girls safe, but he hadn't engineered them for violence. One by one, his projects would fall, and then his daughters would die.

"On second thought, maybe you can. Go back to bed. I'll have a surprise for you in the morning."

CHAPTER SEVENTEEN

What kind of father takes his girls to war? This one. Call child services if you like, but first tell me where my daughters would be safer when a superhero was hunting them. I wasn't letting my children become the nightly news.

"HERT! I NEED another crystal focus." Pre-dawn light refracted off the necklace in Evan's hand. Sweat stained his previously flawless suit.

"Sir, we don't have any other crystals. Not even small ones."

"Then break the one in the Election Machine!"

There was a little gasp.

Evan turned to his minion. "What?"

"We'll never find another piece of holmium that size by next week, sir, let alone calibrate it in time."

He stilled as his mind raced. Everything he had ever wanted dangled in front of him, but now the road forked. He could have the world, or he could have Tabitha. Evan looked at the purple bulb of serum on his worktable sitting next to the four necklaces with magnetic shields meant to protect the girls. There were five people in the world who truly mattered. Losing even one of them would kill him. "Break the Election Machine down. We don't need it anymore."

Hert's bulbous eyes squelched as they blinked. "Yes, Master," he said in a doubting tone.

The door to the basement squeaked open. "Daddy?" Blessing walked down the creaking wood stairs. "Daddy, what is that?"

"This is a little machine that's going to keep you safe." Evan pushed back from his worktable with a smile.

"Safe from what?"

"Crazy people, flying trees, dropping houses, speeding bullets. Anything with mass. I meant to give one to Mommy, but since she's working, I de-cided to make one for each of you girls first."

Four miniature pieces of defensive technology lay in a row on the worktable. If he did decide to give up a life of crime, he could probably sell the prototypes to the US military for a reasonably sized fortune.

"They aren't very pretty, are they?" his daughter asked.

"No, not really. I haven't gotten that far."

Blessing poked at one. It scooted away from her finger before she could touch it.

"Magnets," Evan explained. "Once you have it on, it should repel everything away from you. Right now, they're repelling everything away from the table. I need to find a better power source." Kinetic energy was his first choice, with a backup battery of some form.

The other three girls wandered into the basement, joining Blessing in giving his work skeptical looks.

"Why do we need this?" Angela asked.

Evan sighed. He put his tools down and tried to find an answer. There wasn't a good one. "Mommy is undercover."

"We know that," Maria said.

"And she's run into a little trouble."

Angela smirked at her sisters. "I told you so."

"Daddy is going to help Mommy out. While I'm doing that, I need to keep you girls safe. I'm making you some shields. You will wear these while the minions watch you and Daddy helps Mommy."

"I want to help Mommy," Maria said.

Evan smiled. "That's very sweet of you, but this is grown-up stuff."

Maria's eyes narrowed. Little sparks of solar heat coalesced around her. "I want to help Mommy!"

"We can be superheroes too," Blessing said. "I can fly, just like Mommy."

"Uh huh." Evan nodded. "Except the people Mommy is having trouble with are, technically, superheroes." The girls stared in shock. "They've gone rogue," he explained.

Delilah wrinkled her nose. "Then we can be super villains."

"Not a good idea!" Evan sprang to his feet in alarm. "It's not safe. Very, exceptionally, really not safe. I can't begin to describe how not safe that is." He took a deep breath and looked down at his little girls. They were children. Little children. "Shouldn't you be playing with dolls?"

Maria rolled her eyes. "We won't get hurt, Daddy. You'll protect us. You never got hurt as a super villain, did you?"

"Um..."

"See? We'll be safe."

Delilah raised her hand.

"Yes?"

"Can we have costumes?"

He was blindsided with nowhere to run. "Sure. I'll have a minion get right on that. You do realize that if I let you near a fight, your mother will kill me. She will skin me alive. Literally. This is a very bad idea."

"Mommy doesn't like you leaving us alone either," Maria said.

"Minions don't count," Angela added.

Hert gave him a sympathetic look. "I'm afraid

the genetic programming on these specimens is flawed, Master.”

Evan collapsed back into his chair with a sigh. “Control models, Hert, they never do what you want them to.”

CHAPTER EIGHTEEN

In the end, the minion programmed for color and spatial coordination was given an hour to watch What Not To Wear, *a credit card, and free run of the local sewing shop. The girls talked dresses, designed costumes, and I changed the defensive shields to match Locke, Rage, Strike, and Curse, the newest super villains in the world's pantheon.*

Delilah was my perfect walking Lockpick, all jazzed up in a Victorian suit of copper and black. We added ruffles to the sleeves, and a little top hat. I turned her shield into a watch and she was ready to unlock every secret in existence.

Angela, who could manipulate emotion, chose Rage as her name. She could make people happy, but as a villain, she was going the other way. I dressed her like a young Harry Dresden in a black leather duster, a black fedora, and armed her with a small walking stick. Instead of the pentagram Harry wore, I gave her a heart inscribed in a star for her defensive charm.

Maria became Strike, a dark princess with velvet gown, puffy sleeves, and a choker that held a black gem covering the shield. Very much what I pictured Galadriel wearing if she took the One Ring.

Last of all was Blessing, who changed her name to Curse. We went for a mystic-in-the-desert look with a red robe and hood, except we split the skirt and gave her tennis shoes so she could run.

I never believed in impractical body armor, despite how much I love it on Tabitha.

THE GIRLS RAN around the small backyard, throwing fire at the minions and practicing shielding against water balloons.

Evan held up his last trinket against the setting October sun: a dark gray handgun. The Neanderthals who called themselves superheroes would never realize the true threat the weapon represented—at least he hoped so. Feeling a twinge of fatalistic ennui, he loaded everyone into the minivan. Hert strapped himself into the passenger seat.

"Are we clear on the plan?" Evan asked.

"Yes, Daddy," the girls chorused. At least it was Halloween. They didn't look too out of place.

Yet. He glanced at Hert.

"Yes, Master. The minions are in place. The area has been fully explored and we've set up the 'distraction' for local law enforcement."

Running a hand over the lump in his pocket, Evan took a deep breath. "Very well then. Ladies, let's make this a night to remember."

The twenty minute drive to the warehouse district where the minions had tracked Tabitha to lasted just long enough for Evan to regret everything he planned to do, but not long enough to think of an excuse to back out. He parked across the street and adjusted the cuffs of his Dior suit. "Hert, send in team one."

With a curt nod, Hert sent the outer perimeter team of minions scrambling into place.

"Ladies?" Evan twisted in his seat so he could see the girls, their costumes squashed by their booster seat straps. "You stay with Hert. Move to the upper deck, and locate Mommy. Blessing—"

"Curse," she corrected from under her red hood.

"Of course, excuse me. Curse, you take this, and drop it on the floor in front of Mommy." He handed her a round sphere of purple glass with the antidote to the lotus poison. "The fog from that should clear Mommy's head. Then I want Strike to lay a line of fire between everyone in the building and Mommy. It's okay if I'm on the other side. Rage?" He looked over at Angela. "Keep them confused. And, Locke, you keep the doors open. Once Mommy is with you, get back to the car. Don't stop for anything. "I'll go in and keep them distracted."

And it would probably hurt. But how else could a man prove his love? He stepped out of the car, snagged his sunglasses, and gave himself one last look in the side mirror. Devastating. Doctor Charm, dressed to break hearts. "Give me five minutes to get their attention, then start the fireworks. Hert, keep them safe."

"Yes, Master."

Striding across the empty road, Evan tried to remember the logic behind this insanity, if there'd been any in the first place. Save Tabitha, keep the girls safe.

At least the goal remained beyond reproach. Alas, noble didn't mean *actionable*. So he was winging it. Taking it on the fly. And really hoping he'd get a chance to punch the Rainbow Dane in the balls.

The door swung open with ease. All the superheroes had assembled, dressed in full costume this time. To an outsider it probably looked like a regular Halloween party—if you ignored the fact that the punch smelled of lotus flowers, everyone looked tense, and the conversation was less than convivial. Phrases like, "Kill them all, it's doing the world a favor," floated past and made his blood boil.

Angler Girl nodded to him vaguely, as if she couldn't quite place his face. Rolling Shock scowled in confusion and whispered something to the Rainbow Dane.

Hempman pivoted. "Doctor Charm? Where?"

Evan smirked. They deserved everything he was here to dish out.

The Rainbow Dane turned around. "You?" he roared. "What are you doing here?"

"Me?" Doctor Charm asked with an easy laugh. "I was in the neighborhood. The Peerage asked me to stop by to welcome you to town." He held out a hand to the Rainbow Dane.

The Dane scowled. "Who are the Peerage?"

"Why, my dear boy! The Peerage are the criminal royalty. The movers and shakers of the underworld. I must say, we are all very impressed with this scheme of yours. So original. One hundred percent shock value. I, myself, am merely a plotter. I don't do the violent crimes. I find it ruins your suits. Blood stains on Dior? You can imagine the dry cleaning bill. But this? Dane! This is perfect. Deliciously evil. You are to be congratulated." Doctor Charm mimed doffing his hat as he gave the Dane an elaborate bow.

The Dane wrinkled his nose. "I don't know what you're talking about."

"Why, the murder of all those innocent children. Quite ingenious. You'll be the most wanted man for decades to come." Doctor Charm turned to a passing superheroine in a frighteningly short skirt. "I say, old chap, are all of these delicacies for your enjoyment, or would you mind if I took something home with me?"

Starlit Starlet, stunned by his boldness, stopped to gape.

Doctor Charm lifted her hand to his lips. "*Enchanté*, madam. May I have the pleasure of your company this evening? Do say yes."

Overhead light winked off his watch.

"Y-yes," she stammered.

"Charming, absolutely charming." He tucked her arm into his. "Have a fabulous evening, Dane. Remember, the Peerage is only a call away if you ever need some advice."

The Rainbow Dane stamped the floor, enraged.

Time was running out. The superheroes were stunned now, but in a few moments they'd shake off the stupor and attack. "A tip, gratis: the name will have to go. The LGBT community has never fully embraced the villains of the world and you don't want a lawsuit from them over the use of the rainbow when you start murdering children. Come to think of it, I suspect the Danish will be highly incensed when you start portraying them as wanton killers. A name change will do you a service all round. If nothing else, you need to let the public know that you've changed sides."

"*I am a superhero!*" the Rainbow Dane screamed.

Doctor Charm laughed. "Naturally. Naturally. A superhero who murders children. Isn't he a gem?" he asked Starlit.

The Rolling Shock pushed forward. "We aren't murdering innocent children."

"No?" Doctor Charm smiled. "That's not what I heard."

"We're stopping the children of super villains, and super villains themselves."

He laughed. "The children of super villains? Oh my. Do you know how many super villains have children? Anyone?" He scanned the crowd for an answer. "Anyone at all? No, and rightly so. Super villains don't have children. It's called a condom. We keep things under wraps. Now, superheroes? *You* have children."

There was a gasp from somewhere in the crowd.

"All those adorable little tykes dressed up this evening as they go begging door to door. I suspect there's even one or two dressed as Doctor Charm. They'll make easy targets for the Dane here, and you have no way of knowing who they belong to."

"Super villains have children!" the Rainbow Dane shouted.

"Really?" Doctor Charm caught the hand of another passing heroine. "Stay with me, darling," he whispered.

Zephyr Girl stepped closer. She'd added a small blue mask to her costume, but otherwise looked unchanged.

He tried not to show how much it hurt to look at her.

"The Rainbow Dane is leading us on a noble quest."

"Zephyr? Is that really you?" Doctor Charm leaned forward. "Not so girlish anymore. A bit of weight gain? A pregnancy or three perhaps? I hear you have a boisterous husband back home, or was that a rumor?"

Tabitha's back went stiff.

"She doesn't have any family," the Rainbow Dane said. "She has—what in the blue blazes is that?" He pointed up to the ceiling. Doctor Charm cocked his head at the lights, ignoring the floating purple glass. "Light bulbs. Invented by Thomas Alva Edison in 1879. They turn electric energy into light waves. Really quite an ingenious design, but not new. You've never noticed them before?"

"I meant the purple bulb, you frakkin idiot!"

"Frakkin?" Doctor Charm laughed. "You need to stop watching science fiction shows. I don't see any purple dots. Perhaps it's time to get your eyes checked? Ladies, shall we leave? I fear our host is less than Charming."

The women hanging on his arms tittered appreciatively.

The Rainbow Dane roared, ready to charge, and the anti-lotus bomb dropped. Purple smog filled the air around Tabitha.

"Zephyr Girl! Get away!" the Dane shouted.

Tabitha coughed, but started moving backward, her heels dragging on the floor.

Time to move the party to the next level. Evan was wondering when Maria—Strike—would lay down the cover fire when a voice boomed out. "You stole my mommy!"

Rage and anger made his blood boil. He wanted to break heads, rip the stone from the foundation.

He shook his head and focused on not listening to Angela's mental suggestions.

Overhead lights burst, falling from the ceiling as sparks of flame encircled the room.

"Time to leave. Ladies, it was a lovely thought. Another time perhaps?"

"Who are you?" the Dane demanded.

Evan turned to see him pointing at the girls. Frozen in terror, he barely noticed Hempman closing in on him.

"I'm Rage," Angela said.

"Strike."

"Curse."

"Locke," the other girls said, all posing. "You stole our mommy. You want us dead. Now, you face your choices."

Terror swept the room like a living thing. People dropped to their knees crying. Burning embers rained down at Strike's command, sending people shrieking as they batted at singe marks in their polyester costumes. Doors opened, and people babbled nonsense as Locke let loose.

The Rainbow Dane shook it off and charged. "Abomination!"

Evan dove to intercept, but Hempman knocked him to the ground.

"No!" Zephyr Girl rose up, punching the Dane and sending him flying.

"Those are monsters, Zee," the Dane growled.

"Those are my daughters. The only monster here is you." She wavered on her feet, not fit for a fight.

Evan pulled his arm back sharply, slamming his elbow into Hempman's nose. With a twist, he broke free and had his gun pointed at the Rainbow Dane. "Don't move."

The room stilled.

"Or what?" the Dane mocked. "I'm a superhero, what are you going to do? A bullet won't hurt me."

"This isn't loaded with bullets. One shot, and you're a normal human being. No super power. No abilities. No protection."

Dane rushed him, and he pulled the trigger.

Sneering, Evan side-stepped the enraged superhero. "You'll never touch anyone again. You're normal now. Average. There's nothing heroic about you."

The Rainbow Dane floundered. He staggered forward, and fell to the floor gasping in panic.

The Rolling Shock jumped him.

He pulled the trigger. "Join your friend. Be average. Be nobody. Be forgettable."

Evan risked a glance at the causeway above. Tabitha and the girls were gone. "Superheroes and heroines of varying sizes, it's been a delight to thwart you this evening. Please remember me for all your future vanquishing needs, because—if you touch my family again—there won't be a single superhero left in the world." Doctor Charm bowed.

A swirling opera cape would have added a nice touch.

Silence met his threat. Doctor Charm walked away, confident as only a super villain holding all the cards could be.

After closing the warehouse door, Evan sprinted across the street to the van. Hert was helping the girls buckle. All four were slumped in their seats, barely interested in their bags of Halloween candy.

Tabitha leaned on the side of the van looking lost and confused. "What happened?"

"You were given a lotus serum. It interrupted communication between your synapses and blocked your memory." Evan brushed a loose hair from her face. All his fears fluttered away. Tabitha was back.

"And the fog?" she asked, taking off her mask. Turning it over in her hands, she dropped it to the ground.

"A clarifying agent. It'll pull the lotus serum out of your blood stream. You'll probably have to pee like crazy in an hour, and you might get sick, but your memory will come back."

"Everything seems like a dream. I can't remember what's real and what isn't." Tabitha rubbed her arm, shivering. "Are you real?"

"Always."

Evan helped his wife into the car. She was thinner than he liked, and purple bruises under her eyes marred her perfect face, but she was still beautiful.

If only he knew if she was really coming back to
him. He kissed her forehead.

Glancing back to make sure Hert and the minions were loaded, he sighed. "Let's go home."

CHAPTER NINETEEN

What's it like to fight a superhero? Picture an enraged bull with the intelligence of a monkey and the survival skills of a cockroach. Then think of a way to defeat them. The only option is to outsmart them. That's what I did. A room full of superheroes and I was the only one with my brain turned on.

There is no Peerage, so don't go looking for them. Super villains are self-centered as gyroscopes. We don't play well with others. We don't cooperate. If we did, we'd run the world.

There is no cure to being a superhero. No one knows what makes one person a hero and another an ordinary person. Obviously super strength and flight aren't average skills, but in the grand evolutionary scheme of things, are they that impossible to accept?

And even if we knew what caused the abilities, would I have any right to "cure" someone of being who they are? That's like saying I have the right to 'cure' a person of being

Irish, or African, or religious, or gay. You don't have to like what a person is to accept them as they are.

I hate superheroes, and for a moment, I even considered killing the Rainbow Dane. He stole my wife. He tried to murder my children. But who am I to say who lives or dies? So I left the gun with bullets in my ankle holster and shot him with an extra strong persuasion ray. Nothing changed physically, he was just hypnotized into believing he's average. It's such a simple lie, one almost everyone believes.

Maybe someday I'll start shooting people with the persuasion ray and telling them they're heroes.

THEY STOPPED TWICE, once so Tabitha could pee, and the second time so she could throw up. Somewhere in the middle of Oklahoma, she woke up and stared at him.

"Feeling better?" he asked.

"A little." She rubbed a hand over her shoulder. "What happened to the girls?"

"They grew up. Full into superpowers. Just like their mommy." Evan tried to smile, but there was too much tension. He drove in silence, waiting for her to tell him what she was thinking.

Tabitha cleared her throat. "I don't remember what I did."

"It doesn't matter."

"It does to me."

He let her fall back asleep. The memories would return. It would take time, patience, but they would come back. They rolled into the driveway as the morning sun started to pink the sky. He carried the girls in one by one, tucking them into their beds with a kiss on the forehead. Then he carried Tabitha to their bed. She didn't move as he laid her down, and he dampened a desire to check her pulse. She was breathing. She was home. For now, that was enough.

It should have taken fourteen hours to get from the college campus back to the house. The real house, with a good lab and the broken Morality Machine. Evan did it in five. Tinkering with a mini-van's engine was not illegal, although the speeds he reached probably were. But the police had more interesting things to do with their time, like figure out why every car on the road from Colorado to Texas decided to pull over for a few hours.

Evan stretched out beside her as light filtered through their dark blue curtains, washing the room in deep jewel tones. This might be all he had, this moment of peace with her. When she woke up in the morning, would she love him? Old insecurities wrapped around him tight as a boa constrictor. Could she love him? Could anyone love him?

Tabitha sighed, rolling in her sleep so her head rested on his shoulder, an arm casually flung across his stomach.

It didn't matter if she loved him. He loved her. He always had. He always would. Content, Evan settled beside his wife and fell asleep.

A shriek and the sound of glass breaking in the kitchen woke him up. Tabitha sat up in bed beside him, still wearing her Zephyr Girl costume under a faded t-shirt he'd found wadded up in the back of the van.

"Morning, beautiful."

She raised a skeptical eyebrow at him and scooted away. "Tabitha!" His plea came out too desperate.

"I feel like I haven't showered in days. It tastes like something died in my mouth. Lemme get a shower before we talk."

He sighed. "I don't want to talk," he muttered as she walked away, hips swinging. Grumbling, he kicked himself out of bed, sent the girls to watch TV with a box of cereal, and cleaned up the broken bowls.

When Tabitha came out with wet hair, dressed in old sweats and a t-shirt he'd bought her as a joke when the girls were born that read, 'I make milk, what's your superpower?', the girls were asleep in front of the TV, still worn out from their late-night adventure. It was a perfect opportunity to slip back to the bedroom and make up for lost time. If only she were willing.

Her face was emotionless, no repelling glare, but no come-hither smile either.

Evan's shoulders slumped and he turned away. At least the minions would talk to him.

"Where are you going?" Tabitha asked.

Wondering why she would ask the obvious, he stopped by the door. "Downstairs."

Her hand rested light as a butterfly on his arm. "Are you angry with me?"

"No. Why would I be?" He caught her hand, horrified that she would even think that.

"Because I ran off with another man?"

He shook his head, emotions churning in his stomach. "You were kidnapped. It's not the same thing."

"Then why won't you look at me?"

Evan lifted her hand and gave it a gentle kiss. "Do you want me to look at you?"

She pulled away. "I'm not sure anymore. I'm..." She sighed. "I'm not sure who I am. I'm not sure what I did."

Anger boiled back up from the depths of his psyche. "Did Thane touch you? Did he force himself on you?" Making the Rainbow Dane believe he was average would be enough to protect Tabitha and the girls, but if the Dane had hurt her, Doctor Charm would expand his repertoire beyond basic conniving to outright murder.

Tabitha stared unseeing at the wall for a moment, then shook her head. "No. He stole my memories, he confused me, lied to me, but he didn't..." She trailed off waving a hand. "Thane locked a part of me away, and now I don't know who I am." She sat down, watching the sleeping girls. "I think I need some time to sort it all out."

"I'll go down to the lab then, give you some space to think. We can talk later." Evan let her hand go. If he couldn't make the world perfect, at least he could give her the space she wanted.

"Do you think space is what I need? Evan, I'm adrift." She walked over to their daughters and tucked a blanket lovingly around Maria's shoulders. "What kind of parent forgets they have children? Can a good wife really forget she's happily married? I'm a superhero! And..."

"And you lost. It happens. We all lose some days." Evan kept his voice flat. Admitting he was out of his depth and lost wouldn't change anything.

"I did something wrong," Tabitha hissed. "*Wrong*. How can I keep going from there? How do I know I'll make the right choice next time? I don't know how to live with doubt. I feel empty inside. Everything I was is gone." She stood in the living room looking small for the first time. "I'm empty."

"We'll work it out." He headed for the lab again, and Tabitha followed him down.

"What do you think is down here that will make me better?" she asked as she picked her way through the mess of stuffed animals and destroyed cassette tapes.

He hesitated. Time for truth. "This." Evan pointed to the Morality Machine. "It, ah, tweaks your normal levels of uprightness and makes you a little more, um, horny. For lack of a better term. Sex fixes everything?"

Tabitha ran her hand over the broken machine. "I love your lab." She smiled shyly, and then it turned sly. "Minions, out!"

The multicolored minions peeked out from their various hiding places, large eyes bulging in confusion.

"You knew about the minions?" Evan demanded. They ate grass clippings and occasionally nachos, so there wasn't even a food bill for them. "My mother doesn't even know about the minions!"

With a giggle, Tabitha rolled her eyes. "I met Hert the same night I met you."

"Yes, but I told you I got rid of them!" he shouted over the sound of a hundred flapping feet.

"Lock the door on your way out!" Tabitha called after them. She gave him a patient, one eyebrow raised look. "You are charming and sincere, but not a very good liar, dear. Little things are noticeable. Like the perfectly trimmed lawn when we don't have a lawn mower. Not to mention the actual minions all over the building last night. They don't blend in with the scenery as well as you think."

Huffing, Evan folded his arms. "I told you we had a lawn service."

"Yes, dear, and I'm the one that pays the bills. I know I'm an adult who wears spandex in public, but that doesn't mean I can't add two and two together to make four."

There was an ominous click from upstairs as the last minion filed out and locked the door.

Tabitha turned to him with a sultry smile. "From the first time I saw you in here, all I could think about was having sex on one of the machines. I thought I'd lost my mind."

"Um..." He looked at the Morality Machine. Had the minions fixed it overnight?

"How does this one work?" Tabitha asked as one elegant hand caressed the machine.

He scrambled to form coherent sentences. It was almost impossible when she smiled like that. "Ah..."

She hit him with her best come-hither look. "Is it magnets like the rest?"

"Ah, mostly." Evan nodded, grateful for the easy out. The room was suddenly a lot warmer than usual.

Tabitha laughed. "You're right. I feel better."

Evan blinked. "What'd I miss?"

"It's a magnet, love."

"Yes. An effective one at that. Remember the second time you came to my lab?"

"Vividly."

"I turned this on, and instead of you breaking me into pieces we eloped. And had wild sex six times that night."

"Seven."

"Which is almost the polar opposite of killing me."

"Evan? For a smart man, you really are remarkably dense sometimes. I told you I came to have wild sex and start a scandal that would keep the tabloids talking for decades."

He nodded. "After I turned on the machine."

She shook her head. "How do you think I fly? I use magnetic power all the time. I'm immune to your machines. That's why I could fight you when no one else could."

"Um... You wanted to... with *me*?" The possibility that Tabitha wanted him for himself had never crossed his mind.

Tabitha's eyes went wide. "Who wouldn't? Evan, you're gorgeous! You're on posters. You have a fan club. Have you never read the fan fiction? I used to read it and laugh. Until I met you." She sighed dreamily. One delicate hand touched his face. "How could I not want you, Evan?" She pressed against him.

He held her there as he fell in love all over again. "Because you're perfect? You deserve someone as wonderful as you are."

"And I have you, don't I?" Tabitha tilted her head back, begging for a kiss.

"Always." Leaning in, he captured her lips. She tasted soft and sweet and exotic. She was everything he'd ever wanted, and everything he'd been missing. And they made love on the broken machine that he'd never needed at all.

Evan Smith (Super villain, RET.) teaches ethics and genetic engineering at the University of Colorado. He lives in the foothills with his beautiful wife, four daughters, and is currently expecting his first son.

CLAIM YOUR FREE EBOOK!

Thank you for buying this book!

When you buy an Inkprint Press book in print, we like to thank you by offering you the ebook for free. Please head to:

www.inkprintpress.com/sfrom/
heroesandvillains/love/

and use the coupon EVPRINT to download your free copy in both .mobi and .epub formats. (The coupon will only work once.)

ABOUT THE AUTHOR

Liana Brooks was born in San Diego, California. Years later she was disappointed to learn that The Shire was not some place she could move to, nor was Rider of Rohan an acceptable career choice. Studying marine biology so she could play with sharks seemed to be the only alternative. After college Liana settled down to work as a full-time author and mother because logical career progression is something that happens to other people. When she grows up, Liana wants to be an Evil Overlord and take over the world.

In the meantime, she writes sci-fi and SFR in between trips to the beach. She can be found wearing colorful socks on the Emerald Coast, or online at www.lianabrooks.com.

CHAPTER ONE

Dear Mom,

New York is everything I hoped it would be. I love this school! Last semester alone the students showed a marked improvement over the previous year. And, so far, we haven't had a single senior drop out. This might be our highest graduation rate ever.

I'm really excited by all the improvements. It makes me feel like I'm actually doing something useful. I'm in control of myself, and it's wonderful.

The date with Simon was less exciting. He's... um... "Dull as a brick" might be the right term. You'd think it would be easy to find someone who could carry on an intelligent conversation in New York, especially with Internet dating. It's 2032! But, no, this hypothesis has been proven incorrect yet again.

Give my love to Daddy, Gideon, and the minions. If Maria stops by, tell her I'm worried about her. Delilah and I talked about staging an intervention. I'm not sure, but Delilah thinks Maria will calm down once the shock of losing Martin is over. It may be just a phase.

Oh, and Blessing wrote me. She's in South Africa and loving it. She sent the most hideous picture of a giant bug ever. I forwarded it to Gideon. And I told her not to bring it back no matter how much she adores its fangs.

   Your loving daughter,
   Angela

APRIL IN NEW YORK City. Angela could almost taste the coming summer. She'd even rolled the car windows down to take advantage of the first warm day while she drove back from lunch. Summer would be bliss: eight weeks kid-free that she planned to fill by maxing out her tourist quota and hitting every landmark in a day's drive. By the time her second year as a teacher began in August, she would know more about New York than any native-born city slicker.

Angela parked her car and rolled the windows up. The school was experiencing an unprecedented surge in academic reform, but that didn't mean she needed to tempt the alumni with an easy steal.

A police siren screamed in the distance, echoing the fear and despair radiating from the school. It felt like the first edge of trouble, a nudging headache that made her want to snarl despite her good mood—but New York was like that, the underlying anger of the citizens scraping against her nerves until she was emotionally raw.

Public School 84 was hers though. Angela had been there long enough that she'd been able to slowly shift the mood of the school from fearful resentment to an amiable interest in learning. It was probably just a schoolyard punch-up, nothing to worry over too much.

Sipping on her smoothie, Angela headed for the impressive security array that divided the outside world from the inner sanctum of PS 84. Outside there were guns, drugs, and chaos. Beyond the arch of metal that scanned for everything from weapons to lethal viruses, there were regimented schedules, dusty dead-wood copies of Shakespeare's sonnets, and young minds ready to argue over every word she said.

One of her favorite students had spent an hour debating the merits of shoelaces. You couldn't buy that kind of doublethink.

The security guard wasn't at her usual place in the main lobby, but Angela knew the drill. She swiped her ID, scanned her fingerprint, and headed for the lunchroom where there was undoubtedly a fight emerging.

As she neared the cafeteria, however, fear washed over her like the noxious smell of a skunk in the dark. Angela tossed her unfinished smoothie in the trash and thought of pleasant things. Blue-bonnets on the Texas prairie, the smell of hot apple cider on a crisp winter night, the laughter of her baby brother, the love of her parents... She took it all, wrapping it into the idea of what her school should feel like.

At first, the collective mind of the students fought back. They were scared, and fear was a familiar friend. But she pushed, and they swayed under her will. Manipulating emotions was right up there with the ability to generate polka dots on a wall in terms of usefulness; unless she wanted to turn people into mindless slaves, there was very little she could do as far as the government was concerned. Besides, brute force wasn't her style.

Influencing things was different though. This is different, she told herself. She turned the corner into the cafeteria and almost jumped at the sight of Travys Freeman—top student in her AP calculus class—holding a gun.

The security guard had her Taser out and was trying to talk Travys into handing over the weapon. Terror so thick it was almost a physical force rolled off Travys. There was no way he would hand over anything to the guard. He wanted to turn it on himself. He just hadn't worked up the nerve. Yet. Waiting would be fatal for someone.

Angela cleared her throat and pushed on the mob. Everyone turned, even Travys. She smiled winningly. "This isn't about the quiz yesterday, is it?" she asked, weaving between the tables.

Travys made eye contact. Big mistake. Eye contact meant she had his full attention, and once she had that, he was hers.

"Travys, I asked you a question."

"It's not about the quiz, Miss Smith." The gun wavered, not quite dropping, but he wasn't sure where to aim.

Angela laid a comforting hand on the security guard's arm. "We don't need an audience do we, Travys?"

He shook his head.

"Miss Netley, why don't you get everyone to class? The bell is ringing," Angela added as the bell marking the end of lunch rang out. The crowd stayed frozen, spellbound by the same power that kept Travys from pulling the trigger. It was risky, but she refocused, encouraging everyone to hurry away. "Everyone go to class. Not you, Travys. I want a word with you."

The security guard shook herself out of her stupor. "Come on people, get to class. What are you gawking at?"

Conversation hummed to life around her and Travys sagged. The terror that had buoyed him was gone—only crushing despair remained.

Angela took a seat across the cafeteria table from him as the students and teachers filed out. Some of them tried to stay, or shout, or intervene, but she kept them all walking.

Travys peeked up at her, brown eyes filled with tears. "I'm sorry, Miss Smith."

"Guns don't solve anything. You know that."

He was getting ready to kill himself. She could feel it. The desire to stop the pain overwhelmed him. Angela tried to bleed it off, taking some of the despair herself. It hurt.

"What happened? You can tell me, Travys." She pushed thoughts of safety towards him. He wanted to believe, but Travys had no memories of safety. When they'd first met, he was a failing student, a scrawny sixteen-year-old who flinched when anyone raised their voice. Her power allowed her to create a sanctuary in the classroom, and in that sheltered place, he'd bloomed into a brilliant student.

"Did you get a college rejection letter?" she asked. It seemed the most probable answer.

He jerked his head to the side as if he'd been slapped. "Chris came home."

She sucked in air so fast it whistled past her teeth. "I thought he was doing twenty to life?"

"He got off on a technicality." Chris Freeman was his son's worst nightmare. He was a dealer with an anger problem who saw his only kid as a punching bag. Angela had never met the man, although she'd wanted to rearrange his brain after meeting Travys's mother, a sweet woman who was the poster child for domestic abuse.

"What's your mom doing?"

Travys's eyes dropped to the floor. "She didn't come home from work."

Which made her smarter than Angela thought. "Maybe she didn't know he was coming home."

"She knew."

And crueler than she'd guessed: she'd abandoned her son to a monster. "I'm sorry."

"I'm not going home," Travys said. His thoughts turned back to the gun. Angela could feel his longing for an escape.

"Shooting yourself won't make anything better."

He startled.

"Give me the gun. We'll make other plans for tonight. You won't go back home to him."

Travys hesitated.

"Give me the gun, Travys." She seized at his mind, making him want to please her. The desire for her approval was false—Travys was too strong-minded to need outside approval—but it worked. His arm lifted slowly, like he was fighting gravity.

"You can trust me."

"Nobody move, NYPD!"

Angela jumped. She'd been too focused on Travys to feel the approach of the police. In a split-second decision, she released her hold on Travys and reached out for the minds of the police before they could ruin everything.

It was the wrong decision.

Travys screamed in pain. His hand convulsed around the gun, pulling the trigger, and sending a bullet through the flesh of her upper arm.

Still trying to grasp the collective mind of the police, everything blurred and Angela found herself standing near the main office in the arms of a strange man in bright green spandex.

"Travys! Hold still!" The police were moving, too focused for her to grasp; they'd stunned and cuffed Travys before she could even figure out what had happened.

She tried to brush the man aside. "Let me go." Angela released Travys's mind and focused on herself. The man in bright green held her.

"We need to get you to the doctor," the man said.

Angela realized he wasn't holding her as much as trying to hold her arm. Blood seeped between his gloved fingers. She blinked at it. The pain was secondary to the emotional savaging she'd taken from Travys's mind.

"Stay calm. An ambulance is on the way," the man repeated. He was trying to make eye contact. She didn't cooperate with him.

"I'll be fine. I'd like to check on my students now."

"If I hadn't rushed to your rescue, you would be dead." Confusion tinged his voice, as if he was waiting for praise.

She glared at the team hustling Travys out of the school. "If the police hadn't burst in here screaming, Travys would have handed the gun over and I wouldn't have been shot." She pushed him away. "This is your fault."

"No," said a crisp, authoritative female voice. "This is your fault."

Angela turned to look at the newcomer, an older woman with salt-and-pepper hair and a grim expression, which she recognized from a picture. Katrina Bocks, de facto government employee and chief of the United Nations Council for Superhero Control.

Not a friend.

"Miss Smith, please let the EMT examine your arm, and then I have some paperwork for you to sign."

"What sort of paperwork?" She wouldn't qualify to sign with the teachers' union until she'd worked a full school year, and she doubted the school board was prepared for this kind of situation. Besides, the chances that The Company was involved with something as benign as arranging medical leave were astronomically low. She'd sooner believe in love at first sight.

Katrina gave her a bitter smile, her emotions colored by hate and anger so violent it was almost a physical aura around her. "How long have been aware of your superpowers, Miss Smith?"

Angela played innocent. "Superpowers? I'm a teacher, but that's a generous compliment. Though some days I can't imagine anything harder than twisting these young minds around calculus." She widened her eyes, the very picture of an innocent southern belle.

Katrina wasn't buying it. She held up an old-style thumb drive. "I have papers saying you are a superhero with the ability to perform psychic manipulation."

"I don't believe anyone can do that."

"I also have evidence that you and the young man were in a very unprofessional relationship. When he came to his senses and realized how he'd been used, he came to school to kill you. The public will be incensed to hear you lived." Satisfaction edged Katrina's words. She thought she had Angela pinned in a corner.

The woman had come far too well-prepared. Angela looked over at the EMT hovering behind them. Time for a quick getaway. "I think I need to see the doctor now."

"I'll wait with you," the man offered. "For your protection."

Right, he was her well-meaning bodyguard, another concerned citizen fighting for truth, justice, and the American way. Angela moved to walk past Katrina, then stopped. "How long have you been tracking me?"

"I learned several months ago that a mind-raper was in the area. I didn't know who it was until today."

Angela nodded. Considering they didn't know the name of their target, they had certainly put a plan together quickly. Daddy was not going to like hearing about this. There was always a risk of The Company stumbling across her path this close to headquarters, but things had been so quiet lately she'd been sure she was flying under the radar. "I'll meet you at the hospital, I suppose?"

Katrina smiled triumphantly. "Yes. There's some very simple paperwork you need to fill out. And then we'll discuss more of your future after your surgery."

Her arm stung at the reminder. "I don't think I need surgery, just stitches."

"And I don't think a mutant should be allowed to breed," Katrina said. "Fortunately, the government sees my point of view. A quick snip-snip and you'll be safe to release into the wild."

Angela turned to follow the EMT, teeth clenched hard enough to hurt. There were so many things she wanted to say. None of them would help. Training took over, memories of summer drills under the hot Texas sun. The Company could come at any time. There was no hope of fighting them, so you had to evade, dodge, run.

She let the EMT load her into the back of the ambulance and waited until they'd hit the first stoplight before she dialed the only number that mattered. "Mom, they found me. Come pick me up."

Keep reading:
www.inkprintpress.com/sfrom/
heroesandvillains/movies/